THE DOOMSDAY ARCHIVES

The Heart-Stealer Mask

THE DOOMSDAY ARCHIVES

The Heart-Stealer Mask

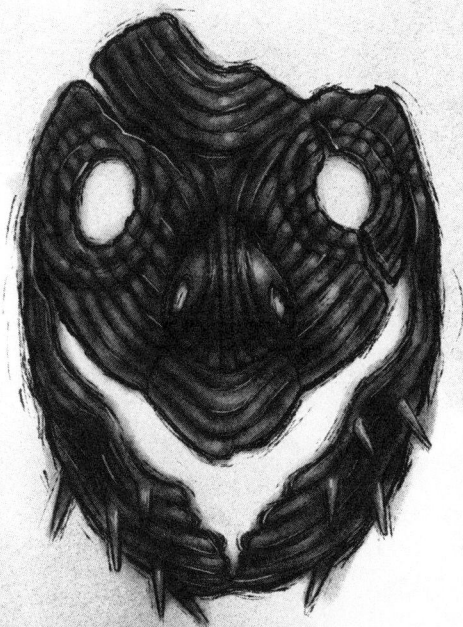

ZACK LORAN CLARK & NICK ELIOPULOS

zando YOUNG READERS

NEW YORK

For Tiffany Liao,
founding member of the Order

PROLOGUE

Clara sat alone behind the register at the Grinning Gas 24-Hour Pumps, playing with one of the novelty fidget spinners and wearing a cheap pair of sunglasses she'd plucked from the nearby rack.

Though it was nearly midnight on a Friday, Clara was working. Not hanging out with her friends, or even sleeping. No, she was here, scrolling through posts of Ashley, Taylor, and Briana all hanging out together, clearly having a much better time than she was.

But Clara wanted a car. No, not wanted—she *needed* one. She was seventeen years old—less than a year away from college. And she was the only one of her friends who didn't already have a vehicle of her own. Without one, Clara would be effectively stranded on the university campus upon her arrival. Even visiting her parents would be next to impossible, unless one or both of them drove to pick her up.

But her parents couldn't afford to buy her a car—not even a used one. Her dad had been laid off recently, and her mom's nursing salary was barely enough to support the three of them.

So if Clara wanted a car, it was up to her to find the money for one.

Clara knew it wasn't fair to resent her folks for their money troubles. They'd worked hard to provide for her. It was a spot of bad luck, and of course there were people who had it way worse than she did.

Still, swiping through the photos of her friends all partying together, she couldn't help but acknowledge the spume of jealousy bubbling up.

It was her senior year. Clara should be celebrating the end of high school, not working late shifts on the weekend to scrape together enough cash for a secondhand junker—one that'd probably break down within a year of her buying it.

She glanced out the gas station's clear glass doors, where a thick wall of mist surrounded the building. This late, Clara always kept the doors locked. It was company policy, in fact. New Rotterdam was quiet after hours. Most folks didn't go out after dark. The town had always had weird stories about ghosts and ghoulies who lurked in the perpetual seaside fog. Dumb superstitions, but plenty of people held to them all the same.

The rare customers who stopped for gas usually paid at the pump and left. The even *rarer* few who needed something from inside she engaged through a tiny window set into the wall beside the register. Her boss, Luke, wasn't a bad guy. He'd told her that as far as he was concerned, the bathrooms were always out of order after 10 p.m.

Still, it was a bit creepy working alone this late. Despite living in New Rotterdam her whole life, she'd never grown completely comfortable with the fog—or the stories of what hunted within it. Stories like the Faceless Founder or the Long-Necked Dog.

Hey you guys want to come to GG? she texted Ashley. *I'm working late again. Free slushies* 😛

Three dots informed her that Ashley was texting back.

Maybe, Ashley responded. *The fog is really bad though. Mom doesn't even want T & B driving. They might stay over.*

After a pause, she added, *You should swing by here when your shift is done.*

Clara sighed. It was an empty invitation and they both knew it. Her shift change was at 5 a.m. Her friends would be long asleep and Clara would be half-dead to the world herself. Her dad would come pick her up and drive her home, where she'd pass out until at least noon.

Most of the cities nearby didn't let teens work this late, but Mayor Selwin Royce had pushed to change the local child labor laws last year. He'd called it "a simple solution to worker shortages and government overreach."

Sounded flimsy to Clara, but this wasn't a forever job. As soon as she graduated, she would pocket the extra cash and run. Or drive, hopefully.

She set her phone down on the counter and glanced out the front door again.

Then Clara let out a startled gasp.

There was something *watching* her from outside. A pale face bobbed in the fog, its features vague and strangely formless. It practically glowed beneath the glare of the gas station's flood beams.

Clara bolted to her feet, dropping the fidget spinner and ripping off her sunglasses. Her hand shot swiftly to the panic button beneath the counter. Pressing it would trigger a silent alarm that alerted the NRPD.

But she hesitated. With the sunglasses now removed, the strange face began to solidify in the mist, its features slowly coming into focus. Clara squinted and realized with a second jolt of surprise that she *recognized* that face.

It was her father.

"Dad?" she said. She glanced down at her phone for any missed messages from her folks. None.

Clara edged from behind the counter, peering through the door. The fog was so thick. All she could see of her father was his smiling face, illuminated by the lights. There was something off about his smile, though. His eyes were glassy and blank.

She slowly approached the gas station doors but didn't unlock them—just gazed out. This felt strange. Wrong.

Then she heard the jingling. It was a cheerful, metallic sound, a bit like ringing bells or—

Or the clinking of keys.

Almost as soon as she'd thought it, her father's body materialized from the fog. Dangling from his outstretched hand was a set of car keys, complete with an electronic fob.

Her dad's smile widened, and he jingled the keys again. It was the most beautiful sound Clara had ever heard.

"No way," she breathed.

Did this mean . . . ? But how? Her parents had informed her in no uncertain terms that she should not expect a car from them. How could they even possibly afford one?

But behind her father there was a sputter of illumination. Headlights flickered on. An engine revved.

Suddenly it was there, parked beside one of the pumps. A gorgeous, brand-new hybrid in goldenrod yellow—Clara's favorite color. The passenger seat window rolled down and there was her mom in her nurse's scrubs, smiling from inside. "Heartbeat Broken" by Infra Red blasted from the radio.

Clara couldn't believe it. The car looked spotless! The paint job was *pristine*. This was *absolutely unreal!*

Her fingers struggled with the heavy dead bolt, but she finally got it open. With a tinkle of the door's chime, she burst outside, into the stifling fog. Clara rushed toward her father, her arms outstretched, ready to wrap him in a hug.

"Oh my gosh—you *guys!*" she shouted excitedly.

But as she was mere feet away, something strange happened. Even stranger than her parents' surprise appearance.

The headlights behind her father suddenly blinked out, and with them the golden yellow hybrid. The car and Clara's mother simply melted into the night, like a cube of sugar dissolving into dark coffee.

A moment later, her father's body seemed to vanish as well, the jingling keys swallowed by the fog.

Clara was inches away now. She skidded to a stop with a yelp. Only her dad's pale, smiling face remained.

And it was a horror.

This was *not* her father, she realized too late. It was something else—some kind of mimic.

In school, Clara had learned about animals that could camouflage themselves by looking like other things. The face looming before her wore a similar disguise. Her dad's features peeled away as she watched, layers of what she'd *believed* was skin unfolding like an insect's chitinous shell. Beneath them, something glowed with a nightmarish light.

It wasn't even a *face* at all, Clara thought wildly. It was some kind of appendage—an *antenna*. And concealed behind it, a sharp, lanky shape loomed close. Waiting. She could barely perceive it in the fog, but she could *feel* it shifting in the still night air. It had stood so still.

The last thing Clara saw was the skeletal figure descending upon her.

She never did get that car.

Boneyards.321 🔒

From the New Rotterdam Wiki Project

Delvedraft is a popular sandbox video game where players explore a blocky, procedurally generated landscape. It's been praised for the freedom it affords players to interact with the game's terrain, creating floating cities, underground complexes, or anything else they might imagine.

In 2018, online rumors began circulating of a secret Delvedraft server. The server, labeled Boneyards.321, was accessible only through an emailed link. An early account of it was made by New Rotterdam Wiki contributor @DelverDave, a fan of the game, on this wiki's Uncanny Sightings page.

> At first it seemed like any other shared server. Shifting day/night patterns, exploding mobs after dark. But then I found the gray city. I've never seen anything like it, and I've been playing DD for years. It was huge but empty. Except for the statues. The city was full of what looked like player avatars. They even had usernames floating above them. But they were all gray and frozen.

DelverDave described an immense cavern beneath the city, with tiles of accumulated bones. He decided he'd explore the underground section another time, but as he was logging out, he recounted seeing an enormous shape in the distance, drawing closer. He disconnected from the server before the shape reached him.

DelverDave planned to stream his exploration of the underground cavern the next night, but his feed cut immediately upon logging in to the server. He never reported back on his second journey. DelverDave's wiki account was eventually deactivated due to inactivity.

Then, three months later, wiki contributor @HatefulKate replied to the buried thread, claiming she'd also received an email with a link to the Boneyards.321 server. She described visiting the gray city from DelverDave's initial post, but with one adjustment— among the frozen avatars dotting the city was one with *his* username.

HatefulKate planned an exploration of her own into the server's subterranean boneyards, but she too went quiet in the days after. Her accounts were eventually flagged as inactive.

1

Interdimensional portals were a challenging field of study. Hazel should know. She was currently studying one.

She stood alone in the Doomsday Archives reliquary, patiently watching its great spire of a doorway. Hazel checked her watch. Just thirty seconds to go.

Part of the difficulty was that magic balked at rules. She'd found this out the hard way in her tests of the various relics housed here. Objects of frequently fabulous and always dangerous power, they were otherworldly land mines that the Order of the Azure Eye had once safely removed from the paths of hapless humans. Until the Order's members were themselves hunted to extinction by mysterious enemies known only as the Yellow Court.

Now it was up to Hazel and her friends—three *kids*—to find and control any new relics that appeared in New Rotterdam, before they could hurt innocent people. And for Hazel, control began with understanding.

Though she struggled with magic, Hazel excelled at learning rules. At school, she studied hard and got good grades, so her teachers liked her. But she was also good in social situations.

Despite being what some might call a nerd, Hazel had never lacked for friends. She'd learned to be friendly without coming off as too eager. Interested, but not intense. And she never spoke about her family's . . . issues.

Still, every time she thought she had a handle on the relics' rules, they seemed to delight in flipping the tables on her. Sometimes literally.

Her own relic most of all.

"Three . . ." she muttered. "Two . . ."

The reliquary door creaked open with a ponderous sound, and there stood Hazel's friend Emrys. He held a worn composition notebook pressed to his chest. Hazel could see his messy bedroom beyond the doorway.

Emrys checked to make sure that his dog, Sir Galahound, didn't follow him in. Then he slipped through, closing the door behind him. Even from this distance, Hazel felt an odd buzz behind her right eye, alerting her to the presence of otherworldly powers at work.

This was the Portam Charm, a wildly useful spell that let them access the reliquary from *anywhere on Earth*. All Hazel and her friends had to do was whisper the incantation in front of a doorway and it would magically open here—to the enclave of the former Order.

Emrys had been the one to teach Hazel and Serena the spell. Of the three friends, he'd been the quickest to find his footing in this strange new reality of theirs. Whatever had happened during his and Serena's encounter with the Wandering Hour relic a few weeks ago—whatever uncanny epiphany had struck him—it had apparently unlocked an intuitive understanding of the occult in Emrys.

Hazel was happy for him. Emrys had always struggled with academics. It was a topic he avoided during their yearly meet-ups at camp, but she'd seen it firsthand when he transferred to Gideon de Ruiter Middle School. As Hazel's mom had explained to her, he was a bright kid with many cognitive strengths, but his ADHD made focus a struggle. In sorcery, Emrys had finally found a subject he excelled at wholeheartedly.

"How long till Serena gets here?" he asked, stepping beside Hazel.

"I told her to come exactly a minute after you," she said, checking her watch. "Then we'll begin the experiments."

"*Experiments*," huffed a third, cantankerous voice. "You needn't bother yourselves with such ridiculous exercises. I know all there is about the reliquary and its thaumaturgic faculties."

Hazel watched as the composition notebook in Emrys's hands twisted and bulged. The marbled black-and-white pattern muddied into ancient brown leather, and an eye drawn into the center in thick blue marker swelled like an inflamed pimple. Two leathery eyelids opened, revealing a single, startlingly *real* eye swiveling in its socket. Where once Emrys had clutched a regular notebook, now a living, blinking grimoire regarded her.

This was Emrys's personal relic, the *Atlas of the End*.

In order to contend with the eldritch forces arrayed against them, Hazel and her friends had each claimed a relic from the Order's stores. Hazel had chosen the Magnus Crown, which contained the fabled philosopher's stone, a mythical item said to be able to perform amazing feats of alchemy, such as turning lead into gold. The Crown also doubled as a cute headband to keep the hair from her eyes, which Hazel wore now.

But while Emrys was already successfully slinging spells with *his* relic, Hazel had yet to successfully turn anything into anything else using the Crown—much less lead into gold. Try as she might, the eerie red stone lodged within the circlet ignored her pleas.

"Magic wants to tell a story," Emrys had once casually explained to Hazel, after yet another failed attempt at catalyzing its powers. "You just have to find your way into the tale!"

Right. Okay. She'll just . . . do that, then.

All the team's personal relics could be disguised as mundane objects when carried out into the world, but Emrys's was special in another way. Because the Atlas also contained the Order's last living member, Alyx Van Stavern. The sorcerer had barely escaped the assassin who'd killed his companions in the Order, magically fleeing into the pages of the spell book.

Now, he was stuck there.

Van Stavern advised his new charges as best he could, but Hazel sometimes found his thinking a bit . . . antiquated.

"Assumptions can distort our observations," she said, turning her gaze back to the doorway. "Especially when we think we know all the answers. No offense to you or the Order, but I'd prefer to draw my own conclusions through fresh eyes and rigorous testing."

"Wow!" Emrys said. "She even countered your big words with vocab of her own."

"Pah," Van Stavern responded huffily. "I know mystical incantations so long they would take lifetimes to pronounce."

"Sounds inefficient," Hazel said. She glanced at her watch. *Three . . . two . . .*

Hazel's right eye buzzed. The doorway opened. Now Serena stood on the other side, her own immaculate bedroom behind her. The three friends lived in the same apartment building, but today Hazel had asked everyone to enter from different places.

The Portam Charm was an incredible gift, to be sure. But Hazel had always been one to immediately look a gift horse in the mouth. What if the horse secretly had razor-sharp fangs or slimy tentacles? They couldn't take anything at face value anymore.

Hazel had questions. Questions she hoped to answer today.

"Usually, I try to be fashionably late," Serena said, sailing through the entryway. "But for you two? I'll make an exception."

Serena had been the most reluctant of the three to take on the Order's responsibilities. Hazel didn't blame her for balking. She and Serena had been friends since they were toddlers, and Hazel knew that behind the breezy exterior there was a shrewd and perceptive mind. Serena had a knack for picking up details that others missed, for seeing the truths buried behind misleading distortions. She didn't like being rushed into hasty action.

And Van Stavern certainly hadn't wasted any time recruiting them. New Rotterdam was in peril. They were his only hope. The forces of darkness were closing in *now*, etc. It was little wonder Serena had refused him at first.

Until those dark forces came for *her*.

Serena now wore her own relic, the Aegis of Truth, as a bangle on her left wrist. In its true form, the Aegis was a lustrous mirrored shield, though Hazel had yet to see Serena use it as such. Still, she wore it everywhere she went. And even without her relic's help, Serena was probably the *most* sensitive of the three to supernatural forces. She was usually the first to notice when something was amiss.

Serena's eyes now settled on the Atlas. "And the book's here, too." She sighed. "Lovely."

"I have a right to observe your rituals," Van Stavern muttered. "Testing the boundaries of otherworldly powers is a dangerous proposition. The more you push agai—"

"See, it's never just *observing*, is it?" Serena said, closing the door behind her. "There's also the talking. So much talking, for a book without a mouth."

"What's next?" Emrys interjected brightly, snuffing the argument before it could truly catch. "Also, I still don't get why we had to come in separately."

"I'm curious about that, too," Serena said.

Hazel nodded. "According to Van Stavern, and our own observations about the Portam Charm, we know it follows certain rules. When a person uses it to enter the reliquary from our world, the spell also generates a return trip for that person—sort of a personal, invisible ticket home—back to whatever doorway they'd entered from. That means we can't use the door to teleport across distances. One entrance, one exit. Always the same door."

Serena nodded slowly. "Okay . . ." she said. "It makes a spooky sort of sense, I guess."

"Except it's wrong," Hazel said. "At least, I think it might be. Because what happens when Emrys enters from his room, and Serena from hers? If Emrys then uses his return trip to open the door back to his room, couldn't Serena just follow him back through the already-opened doorway? Effectively teleporting her across the building?"

Emrys's eyes widened. "Hey—yeah!"

Serena frowned, considering. "Maybe the rules don't work that way. What if the door doesn't let me through?"

"It's possible," Hazel agreed. "But that's what we're here to find out. And imagine how useful it'd be if we're wrong." She nodded to Emrys. "You ready?"

Her friend nodded back. "Sure," he said. Emrys stepped toward the reliquary door, placing his hand around the golden knob enameled with a bright blue eye at its center. He twisted the eye, and the door opened back into his room with a fizz of magical feedback.

Emrys held out his arm to Serena. "Ladies first?"

Serena rolled her eyes. "Benevolent sexism is still sexism," she said. But she walked past him, hesitating only briefly at the doorway before stepping through.

And there she was, standing in Emrys's bedroom. Sir Galahound, stirred by her sudden arrival, hopped to his feet and began whining at Serena's shins. She bent down to scratch behind the dog's ears.

"Emrys, honey," she said. "It's time to open a window. It smells like boy in here."

"Hey!" Emrys said. "Isn't *that* sexist?"

"Like patriarchy, then," Serena said, rolling her eyes again. "Sweaty, stinky, adolescent patriarchy. With a hint of dog."

Emrys stepped through the doorway himself. "Okay, it worked! We made it through."

So, Hazel had been right. Both Emrys and Serena had taken the same return trip to one location, proving that the charm could be used in surprising ways.

"What now?" Serena called through the doorway.

"Close the door and use the incantation again," Hazel said. "Then both of you re-enter the reliquary. That's where we'll test my second theory."

Emrys nodded, taking the door handle from the other side, where it resembled his white-painted closet rather than the dark wood of the reliquary. He closed the door.

A moment later, the door opened again, and both Emrys and Serena entered together.

"So," Serena said, shutting it behind her. "How do I get back to *my* bedroom now?"

"Well, that's where my second theory comes in," Hazel said. "You . . . don't."

Serena blinked at her.

"Using the charm this way has lots of practical applications!" Hazel added hurriedly. "As long as we can get to a door, we can get to *each other*. I could have used it to help you both against Edna Milton, for instance! But my guess is that the return ticket is generated the moment a person steps into the reliquary. And it . . . cancels the previous ticket. One per customer."

Serena whirled around, throwing open the doorway. There was Emrys's bedroom, right as they'd left it. Sir Galahound's tail pounded excitedly.

"*Hazel*," Serena groaned. "My dads aren't home yet, but my brother is. He saw me go into my bedroom and not come out!"

"Just say you snuck by without him noticing," Emrys suggested. "It's Dom. He's not that observant."

"This is a limitation we needed to be aware of," Hazel said. "Because the consequences could be much worse. Tonight, we started just a few apartments away. But what if one of us is on a trip across the country? Using the charm this way can bring us together, but it could also leave us stranded." She held up her cell phone, where the no-signal symbol glowed at the top. "And since pocket dimensions don't come equipped with cell-phone towers, we'll need to coordinate *outside* the reliquary. That's why I asked you to enter at specific times."

"You really thought this through," Emrys said.

"I must admit, even I'm impressed," Van Stavern agreed.

"That's our Hazel." Serena sighed. Then she frowned into Emrys's room, where a gauntlet of dirty laundry blocked her only exit.

Perhaps Hazel should have reversed the order they used the Portam Charm . . . Ah, well. This was a learning process, after all.

"Before we go," Serena said, "did you both see that RotterCon is in a couple weeks?"

Emrys immediately perked up. "Oh—oh wow! I didn't realize it was so soon! Can we still get tickets?"

RotterCon was the local fan festival dedicated to all things horror. People showed up from everywhere in the region, dressed in costumes of famous monsters and notorious cryptids. Many of the most respected contributors to the New Rotterdam Wiki Project attended every year. Some even gave panel discussions on interesting urban legends! Emrys and Hazel had wanted to go together forever, but now that he lived in town, it was actually possible.

Or, it might have been . . .

"There were still tickets as of this morning," Serena said. "And Sunday is the dedicated Kids Day. It's only forty dollars to get in."

"Yessss," Emrys gushed. "We *have* to go, right? I mean, now that we're real-life monster hunters, it's practically a requirement!"

Serena shook her head, but she was smiling. "I guess it's an opportunity to cosplay," she said. "I've always wanted to try a Creeping Ginny costume. The candle should be easy enough, but how to make a wearable window . . ."

"I can't go," Hazel interrupted.

Emrys and Serena both turned to her, their excitement quickly fading.

"Really?" Emrys asked, disappointment clear on his face. "Why not?"

"I have plans," Hazel lied. She could feel herself tensing and willed her expression to remain carefully neutral.

Only forty dollars.

For Emrys and Serena, a forty-dollar ticket may have been nothing. They'd ask their parents for the money and that would be that.

Hazel didn't have that luxury.

She affected an air of casual disappointment, hoping it covered the heartbreak she was really feeling. Hazel had wanted to attend RotterCon for as long as she could remember. Every summer at camp, she and Emrys would pore over the cosplay contest entries from the previous year, noting the panels they would have sat in on. But as Hazel's home life had become more complicated, even small dreams like this began to feel increasingly unattainable.

"Sorry," Hazel muttered. "I told my mom we'd spend that weekend together."

"I'm sure she'd understand," Serena said. "The con only happens once a year, after all."

"I . . ." Hazel paused, shifting her backpack. "I'll see what I can do," she finally conceded. "But no promises."

"Let us know how we can help!" Emrys said. "I'm very good at begging parents for things."

As Emrys and Serena departed the reliquary through his bedroom, Hazel tried to picture herself pleading with her mom for the money. She could already picture the pained expression it would elicit, the shameful apology—and that thought made her own cheeks flush with guilt. It's not that her mother didn't *want* to pay for things like nerdy horror conventions. She just . . . she just couldn't.

But maybe Hazel *could.*

She unconsciously brought her fingers to her hair, where the Magnus Crown now rested. Though she and her friends had finished one supernatural experiment for the day, Hazel's work wasn't over yet.

She'd learn to control the Crown, even if it was the last thing she ever did.

The Tearful Eye Lighthouse 🔒

From the New Rotterdam Wiki Project

No lighthouse is complete without a ghost story or two haunting its stately tower, but the one at Cimmerian Bay has at least a dozen. Dubbed the Tearful Eye by locals, the lighthouse has an infamous history of killing its keepers.

Its original custodians, a husband-and-wife team whose names were only recorded as T. and E. Van Vuren, died just six months into their post. According to historical records at the time, husband T was an aspiring accordionist, and brought his instrument to entertain them during their long, lonely nights. Unfortunately, he only packed the sheet music for a single song. E's diary, recovered posthumously, describes her slow descent into madness as her husband repeated the same piece night after night, until she eventually threw the instrument, her husband, and finally herself into the churning sea.

Delirium was a common theme among those who later took up the post, as the isolation of the job grated on even the hardiest of spirits. The journal of Martin Dalmas, a French immigrant and former sailor, described seeing shapes approaching from the ever-present fog that surrounded the bay, stooped humanoid forms who stopped just short of the lighthouse's beam, but were always waiting. Dalmas was found barricaded in the lighthouse gallery. He'd starved to death, rather than venture outside.

Those who attempted to alleviate the ravages of loneliness by joining with others fared little better. The O'Neille brothers, Cody, Cadan, and Colin, were reportedly as close as could be before they took on the post. Little is known of the brothers' time in the Tearful Eye, as the young men kept no journals. But each died with a makeshift weapon in hand, having apparently struck down one of their brothers as they in turn were killed.

Eventually, improvements in maritime navigation and the invention of GPS made lighthouse keepers obsolete, and the Tearful Eye was converted into a fully automatic system. However, there have still been numerous sightings over the years of shadows moving within the glare of the lantern room.

Some believe that the lighthouse never truly released its keepers, even after they died. And occasionally, those walking the docks of Cimmerian Bay claim to hear a somber accordion playing from the fog.

2

As Hazel closed her closet door, the buzzing behind her eye abruptly stopped. The Portam Charm had run its course, depositing her back into the mundane world—the world of math homework and microwave dinners and evening chores.

Of course, as the keeper of the Magnus Crown, Hazel always had a little bit of the unseen world close at hand. If only she could get her relic to do anything!

Evidence of her frustration with the Crown was piling up on her desk: a disc-shaped paperweight that remained stubbornly lead; an iron bookend that refused to rust at her command, no matter how politely she framed it; a glass of water that, despite what Van Stavern had told her about the Crown's ability to "stitch and sunder molecular bonds," showed no signs of exploding, evaporating, or transmuting into soda.

Magic wants to tell a story. If that were true, Hazel feared she'd already missed the good parts. What if the fabled philosopher's stone had simply run out of juice?

"A whole pocket dimension full of powerful talismans and legendary weapons," Hazel mumbled, worrying the Crown with her hands, "and I picked the six-hundred-year-old dud."

Hazel's turtle, Mary Shelley II, turned her rheumy gaze in Hazel's direction, as if the words had been directed at her. "You're not *that* old," Hazel told her. "I'm pretty sure."

"Hazel, honey?" called a voice. "Are you home?"

Before answering, Hazel cast about her room for anything she needed to keep hidden from her mom. But there was nothing terribly suspicious about a glass of water or a paperweight, and her relic had already disguised itself as a simple headband—so at least it was good for something.

Hazel met her mom by the front door of their apartment as she was kicking off her shoes. Her hands were full—she'd stopped for takeout—so Hazel slid in for a one-armed side hug.

"It's Friday, right?" said her mom. "I made it to the weekend?"

"Friday night," confirmed Hazel. She gestured at the wall calendar as they stepped into the kitchen. The calendar had a Universal Monster theme; this month featured the Bride of Frankenstein, her gaze turned heavenward; although, due to the arrangement of the kitchen, she appeared to be gazing at the microwave with no small amount of longing. Far from monstrous, the delicate stitches along the Bride's jawline only underscored her uncanny beauty. Below the black-and-white photograph, the calendar's grid of dates had been color-coded to reflect Hazel's mom's irregular work schedule at New Rotterdam's largest and busiest hospital. She'd just finished a ten-day stretch of twelve-hour shifts.

"I love it when my weekend happens at the same time as your weekend," she told Hazel. "I want a bubble bath and fried chicken and a movie night with my daughter. I'll even let you pick—"

Hazel perked up.

"—from my *dazzling* collection of romantic comedies."

"Ugh," said Hazel. "Honestly, how many versions of *Pride and Prejudice* does the world need?"

Her mother gave her a playfully withering look. "Says the girl who asked me to take her to the remake of the reboot of *Backwater Butcher VII: The Butchery.*"

Hazel rolled her eyes. "Not even close, Mom."

"Oh, sorry, did I butcher the title?" This elicited another well-earned groan. "Honestly, Hazel, those movies of yours—if you saw some of the things I see at work . . ."

Hazel turned from the open silverware drawer and took a real look at her mom. The skin beneath her eyes looked thin and pale, almost translucent. Hazel could see the little blood vessels, like the blue afterimage that followed a lightning bolt. Her hair, pulled back in a greasy ponytail, was stippled with new flecks of white, like fresh fallen snow. Her scrubs were stained with who-knew-what.

Next, Hazel's eyes drifted over the kitchen. There were still dishes in the sink from two days ago, and the recycling bin was overfull (they'd missed last week's pickup), so empty cans and bottles were lined up on the counter. There weren't any clean forks in the silverware drawer, so Hazel would have to quickly wash a couple before they could eat.

She resolved to thoroughly scour the kitchen after her mom turned in for the night. Hazel didn't want her mom to feel guilty about Hazel taking on so many of their domestic tasks, so she tended to clean out of sight. She didn't mind the chores, truth be told. Cleaning was therapeutic. It gave her a measure of control over her tiny corner of the universe.

But chores and a movie night meant she wouldn't have time to practice with the Crown. Not until late, anyway. Hazel supposed it was her turn to lose some sleep for the sake of the family.

"A rom-com sounds great, Mom," said Hazel. "Really."

Her mom's phone rang while Hazel was at the sink. "It's my shift supervisor," she said, groaning, presumably with good reason. Hazel knew that shift supervisors didn't call to wish their employees a happy weekend.

"Patti, what's up?" said her mom. "No. I'm sorry, but no. I'm sure Dr. Strathmore *is* desperate, given the staffing issues we've discussed, but maybe he should ask that billionaire to hire more staff. I've been on the clock since I don't even know when . . ."

Hazel only vaguely knew the people she was talking about. *That billionaire* was some philanthropist who'd recently given the hospital a bunch of money to renovate its pediatric wing, though none of the money had gone to the ER, where her mom worked.

Dr. Strathmore she was a bit more familiar with. If Saint Azazel Hospital had a reputation for fixing the unfixable, then Strathmore was a large part of that reputation. He specialized in trauma cases, and Hazel's mom frequently spoke in awe of his ability to bring patients back from the brink.

As her mom traced the days on their wall calendar, passing her finger over blue boxes and green boxes and red, Hazel was reminded of the periodic table, the visual tool scientists used to organize the known elements. Hazel straightened as an idea took hold. She had been so caught up in researching famous (or infamous) alchemists—Saint Albert and Nicolas Flamel and Cagliostro—that she'd forgotten her first instinct had been to think of transmutation as a science. As *chemistry*.

Her mom was listening intently to whatever her supervisor had to say, so Hazel figured she had a few minutes to try something. She ran back to her room, and, shoving aside a stack of books on alchemy and mysticism, she set down her science textbook.

Perhaps the key to controlling the philosopher's stone was in starting small. Like, atomically small.

Emrys had said magic wanted to tell a story. Well, Hazel's language arts teachers always taught her that you needed to learn the rules of writing before you could break them. Maybe alchemy was a bit like that, too. Perhaps Hazel needed to begin with a short story before she penned her first manuscript.

She opened the textbook to the dog-eared spread of the periodic table. Just as her mom had done with the calendar, she ran her finger along the colored boxes. This time, she paid attention to the precise locations of various elements.

Lead and gold were on the same row, but there were a couple of elements between them. What in the world was *thallium*? Maybe the fact that Hazel had no idea was part of her problem.

Just above lead was an element she *did* recognize: *tin*. She could picture tin cans, old toys made of tin, costume jewelry . . .

So she held the lead weight in one hand and thought of tin.

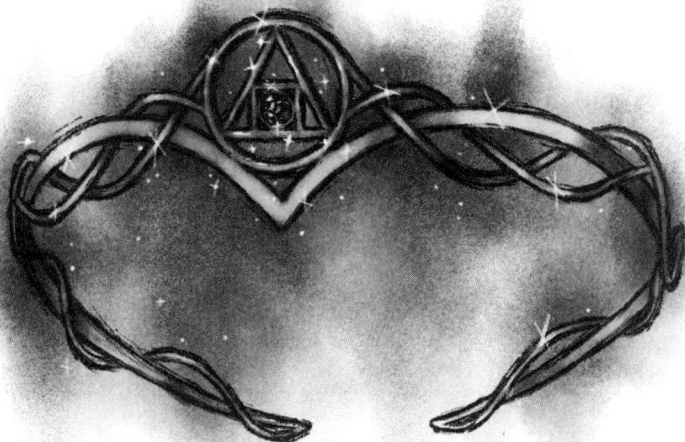

With her other hand, she touched the delicate diadem at her temple. Hazel had half expected it to still be in its camouflaged form. She hadn't noticed it changing.

But she noticed what happened next.

A strange red sparkle glimmered from outside her field of vision—the same brilliant red as the philosopher's stone. For a moment, Hazel thought she felt a *presence*, like a teacher gazing curiously at her work from just behind her shoulder. Though she sat alone in her room, she felt oddly self-conscious.

Then, to her absolute shock, the lead weight in Hazel's hand seemed to shiver and warp, as if it was on the verge of liquefying. It remained solid, however; its rigid shape held, but it grew suddenly lighter—lighter in weight and in color, as, with a glittering flash so sudden it made her blink, the paperweight changed from storm-cloud gray to a dull silver.

A faint electric charge made the little hairs on Hazel's forearms stand on end, and she felt suddenly lightheaded, but the unsettling sensation was forgotten in the wave of elation that followed.

Hazel laughed, gripping the object in both hands. It bent beneath the pressure. That would have been impossible a few seconds ago.

"It's tin!" she squealed, waving it in front of her turtle's terrarium. "Mary, I did it!"

Hazel pored over the periodic table, making a mental inventory of elements she was familiar with. She knew that tin and lead shared a lot of similarities, chemically speaking, since they were in the same column. Lead was composed of larger atoms, with more protons and an additional layer of electrons. Had that been the charge she'd felt in the air? Had Hazel shorn a layer of electrons away from the paperweight's atoms, just by thinking about it?

She should have known. It was just as she'd proven with the portal spell. Even magic followed rules. The philosopher's stone wasn't making something out of nothing; it was altering matter on a subatomic scale.

So if Hazel wanted to make gold, she'd have to come at it from another angle. She looked at the table again to see if she recognized any of gold's elemental neighbors, and she smiled.

"Mom!" she called, hurrying back into the kitchen. "Do we still have that old thermometer? The analog one?"

As Hazel rounded the corner, the sight of her mom stopped her in her tracks. "Mom? Are you . . . crying?"

"Oh, honey, I'm sorry," her mom answered, rubbing the moisture from her cheeks. "It's probably nothing. My coworker Ginny—you remember her daughter, Clara?"

"Of course," Hazel said. Clara had used to babysit Hazel when she was younger. She still remembered her fondly. They watched movies and made cinnamon toast treats together, and Clara usually came bearing candy for Hazel, so long as she promised not to tell her mom.

"Well . . . Clara never came home last night."

Hazel's blood ran cold. In New Rotterdam, someone disappearing overnight was definitely a cause for concern. Hazel knew that better than anyone.

"We're hopeful she just crashed at a friend's place after work, but someone needs to cover Ginny's shift tomorrow if they still haven't found her. That billionaire who built the new wing, Julius Worthmann, is supposed to visit and . . . well, there's no one else." She sniffed, wiping her nose with the back of her hand. "I'm worried for Clara, of course, but I think mostly I'm just tired. I don't even know why I'm crying."

"It's a normal reaction to stress," Hazel answered. "Your body is flooding with hormones, and that can cause crying." She'd read that in a book.

"Well, it isn't doing anyone any good. I've got five hours to eat, sleep, and shower—oh, but my scrubs are filthy." Her lip quivered; it reminded Hazel of the paperweight, in that instant before it transformed. Tentative and watery.

"I can do the laundry," Hazel offered. This wasn't as simple a task as it sounded; the washing machine had been broken for weeks, which meant lugging their laundry down the stairs, across the street, and around the corner to Screamin' Suds. It was a hassle, but Hazel would rather lug a grand piano down those stairs than watch her mom cry.

"You're a good kid," her mom said. "I promise—I *promise*—I will get the washing machine fixed just as soon as your father gets around to paying child support."

"Don't even worry about it, Mom," Hazel said brightly. She darted in to give her mom a peck on the cheek. "Get into your pajamas. I'm just going to finish some homework before I head out, so leave your scrubs by the front door, okay? And maybe Clara will turn up while you're asleep."

Hazel decided to alert Emrys and Serena if she still hadn't appeared by morning. A missing teenager was distressing, yes, but there could be perfectly normal reasons for her to go quiet. Clara was nearly a college student by now, after all. Perhaps, like Hazel's mom suggested, she was just sleeping off a long shift at a friend's.

Besides, Hazel still had one more idea to try with the Crown before she tackled her chores. She found what she was looking for in the hall closet. Her mom had kept some old equipment from her time in nursing school, which Hazel had played with as a kid. There was a stethoscope and a rubber mallet for testing reflexes—and an old-school thermometer, a glass tube containing the liquid metal known as mercury.

Mercury was toxic, Hazel knew, so she extracted it with care, slicing the thermometer open with a glass cutter and letting the mercury drip out onto a ceramic plate. It rolled and beaded along the surface, and she checked the periodic table one last time.

Gold was element number 79, and mercury was 80; it was the difference of a single proton, a single electron. Hazel adjusted the Crown and imagined shedding that electron; in her mind's eye, she flicked it away in a cavalier act of astral-atomic surgery.

There was another strange shimmer of red. This time, however, the presence Hazel had sensed before seemed different.

The invisible gaze that watched her work turned stern, almost disapproving. Hazel felt a dull headache coming on. Her temples throbbed and her thoughts went fuzzy.

Was the Crown . . . resisting her?

She pushed through the discomfort. Perhaps this was a different kind of test. Hazel had resolved to control the Crown's power, and she wasn't about to give up now.

Then, after an excruciating moment of psychic tension, the beads of mercury that had pooled against the plate glowed like iron in a forge—silver to orange to red—before quickly settling on a brilliant yellow color.

The watchful presence withdrew from Hazel's perception, but the headache didn't. If anything, it seemed to be getting worse.

Huffing for air like she'd just run a marathon, Hazel poked the metal with her finger, half expecting it to be hot. But it was cool to the touch—soft but *solid.*

Gold. She'd made gold! Created something valuable and beautiful and rare through sheer force of will.

Hazel felt a sudden rush of exhaustion, a more profound version of the lightheadedness she'd felt before. A lance of pain stuck her stomach. Hunger cramps? Combined with her headache, it was all she could do to keep from falling out of her chair. That couldn't be a coincidence. Hadn't Van Stavern once said something about the Crown tapping into the metabolism of the person who wielded it?

And what was up with that strange feeling of opposition? Moments ago, she'd changed an entire paperweight into tin and barely felt winded. This time, however, just a few small dots of gold had nearly knocked her off her feet. Hazel was oddly anxious about the air of displeasure she'd sensed coming from the Crown. It was a bit like having a teacher be mad at her.

Teachers were *never* mad at Hazel.

Still, gold was gold. She eyed the glittering specks with the hungry eyes of a prospector. This was big. Huge, even. Hazel's first thought was to text Emrys about her victory, but she hesitated.

Perhaps she should sleep on it first. Yes, this was a momentous achievement, but Hazel still needed to think through the best ways to *use* it. Just looking at the screen of her phone made her vision blur with sleepiness. She wanted nothing more than to take a nice, long nap.

Hazel sighed. The nap would have to wait, too. She may have just performed *literal* alchemy in her bedroom, joining the hallowed ranks of the unseen world's occult scientists and rewriting the very laws of thermodynamics . . .

But she still had chores to do. And as far as she knew, stain removal was not among the miracles made possible by the Magnus Crown.

She'd have to ask Emrys if there was a spell for that.

Pumpkin Patrick

From the New Rotterdam Wiki Project

Among the biggest toy crazes to strike New Rotterdam were the 1980s Pumpkin Patrick dolls, a series of characters said to have sprouted from the Happy Harvest Pumpkin Patch every Halloween. Pumpkin Patrick, the titular leader of the Harvest Gang, was accompanied by other fall-themed characters such as Candy Cora, Mack Applejack, and Scarecrow Sally.

The dolls were commonly available in New Rotterdam gift shops, bookstores, and even local groceries during the fall season. Each appeared to be hand-stitched, with cloth bodies and lacquered wooden heads. They were distributed through a New Rotterdam wholesaler, YelloCo, though their original creator remains a mystery.

In 1984, Gladys Brouwer reported that, after purchasing a Pumpkin Patrick doll for her six-year-old grandson, Douglas, she began noticing strange behaviors in the boy. He could be heard whispering to it late at night, and would claim that Pumpkin Patrick spoke back to him, urging him to "come join the harvest dance." Eventually, Douglas was forbidden from sleeping with the doll.

Douglas adored Gladys's snickerdoodle cookies, an annual fall treat that she baked for the neighborhood. In fact, the family nickname for him was Snickerdoodle, both for his love of the cookies and for his long, cinnamon-colored hair. This year, however, the sight of his grandmother's cookies sent the boy into a screaming fit that lasted several hours.

One night, after putting Douglas to bed, Gladys claimed to have heard tiny footsteps on the house's stairwell. Upon investigating, she found the Pumpkin Patrick doll lying face up in the hallway. Next to it, Douglas's bedroom door was ajar, the boy soundly asleep inside.

Douglas Brouwer went missing several days later, disappearing from his bedroom in the middle of the night. The boy was never found. By some strange coincidence, however, a new doll appeared among the Harvest Gang exactly one year later: Snickerdoodle Dougie, with a mop of cinnamon-stick hair.

3

Turning mercury into gold had been one thing, but turning gold into money was another.

If life were a video game, Hazel would simply walk into a shop and hand the beads of gleaming metal over in exchange for whatever she needed. But real life, alas, was a bit more complicated than that. Especially Hazel's.

A quick internet search resulted in a handful of gold and silver buyers in town, but such places didn't exactly advertise their rates. And generally they dealt in antique jewelry, not shapeless droplets brought in by kids. Maybe a pawnshop would be less likely to ask questions? Was there a difference?

Hazel copied down the address and phone number of the closest one, a shop with the promising name of Bullion Buyers.

She hadn't even really acknowledged her plan until it was already underway.

Hazel's mother worked hard. Too hard. After Dad left a few years ago, there had been a series of "belt-tightenings," temporary measures that her mom assured her would be over before she knew it.

And yet the belt never did loosen. Money was a constant anxiety for their small family, an anxiety that Hazel kept hidden tidily away from her friends.

She could still remember the exact moment she'd realized she was *poor*. It was only last year. Serena's whole class at the Academy of the Sacred Silence—the fancy private school she attended—had been tasked with donating gifts for the annual New Rotterdam Holiday Toy Drive.

Serena had spent weeks strategizing over what to donate, hoping to one-up her classmates and provide the perfect present to whatever disadvantaged youth received it. The gift had to be gender-neutral and widely appealing; showy but not ostentatious. She finally settled on a stylish faux-leather backpack, the absolute height of school fashion. And the donation went over just as she'd hoped. Serena was the talk of her class.

Hazel never said so, but she'd coveted that backpack. It was exactly the kind of accessory she'd never be able to afford. It was so elegant and mature-looking—she envied the kid who would receive Serena's generous gift.

Until the day she did.

Hazel's mom had presented it to her on Christmas morning, her face beaming with excitement. She must have been elated to give her daughter such a chic present, after so many lean holidays in a row. Hazel still grimaced to think of her reaction, the quiet horror that her mother mistook for disappointment.

She never wore the backpack, not even once. It was an emblem of shame, a relic every bit as powerful as the ones contained by the Doomsday Archives. It was still buried in the deepest recesses of Hazel's closet, hidden from Serena's all too perceptive eyes.

Hazel knew her friend would never purposefully humiliate her over a lack of money. Serena was the opposite of the spoiled-rich-girl cliché. She was thoughtful and big-hearted, and the best gift-giver Hazel had ever met. She frequently paid for lunches during trips to the Shallows shopping district.

Still, Hazel's shame was a hurdle that she couldn't quite seem to vault. She kept her money troubles as muted as possible, and never invited her friends over anymore.

But what if the Magnus Crown could change all that?

Despite her exhaustion from the previous night's discovery, and the hours she'd spent doing chores, Hazel awoke early the next morning to continue her research, just hoping her mom's ten-year-old laptop didn't crash in the process.

She did a quick search for the price of gold and discovered that bullion recognized as being at least 99.5 percent pure was valued at $70 a gram.

Next, she searched for the average amount of mercury in a home thermometer and learned that they typically carried about a gram themselves, give or take. Hazel didn't have any way to measure exactly how much gold she'd created, but even if it was less, that should be more than enough gold for a ticket to RotterCon.

She grinned through her exhaustion. That was one financial woe down, but Hazel knew she'd need to think bigger if she *really* wanted to monetize the Crown's powers and help her mom.

According to the library books she'd checked out, the philosopher's stone of legend was capable of a number of feats that were far more magical-sounding than the shearing of electrons. The internet mostly agreed. It could mix life-giving elixirs and heal disease. (That certainly sounded valuable. Hazel wrote it down.) It could create ever-burning lamps and turn coal into diamonds. (Which made sense. Both coal and diamonds were composed of carbon. And coal was far more readily available than mercury. A promising lead?)

Albert Magnus—the original bearer of the stone, if Van Stavern was to be believed—had supposedly created a powerful formula called *aqua fortis* ("strong water," Hazel translated through the search engine), which could dissolve any metal *but* gold. Something about that sounded familiar. A quick search confirmed it: *aqua fortis* was another name for nitric acid, an incredibly corrosive chemical. Potent, but not especially lucrative. Still, Hazel was surprised by its simple formula. HNO_3— just hydrogen, nitrogen, and oxygen. Each element was readily available in the air. When thrust together, however, they could melt even steel.

But some ancient alchemists believed that the stone's true purpose—the ultimate call of alchemy, really—was to create *life*.

Hazel frowned as she read a description of a creature called a homunculus. Miniature spirits of clay and fire, they were supposedly the masterworks of powerful alchemists. They sounded sort of like fairies to Hazel, but grown in a lab.

She couldn't imagine why someone would make such a thing . . . aside from the thrill of scientific discovery, of course. Until she read one of the earliest descriptions of homunculi, penned by a man named Paracelsus.

"Through art they are born," she whispered aloud, *"and therefore art is embodied and inborn in them, and they need learn it from no one."*

Supposedly such creatures had any number of fabulous arts at their disposal. Inborn knowledge about the nature of the universe, up to and including the ability to see into the future. Wow. If Hazel knew the lotto numbers ahead of time, maybe she could convince her mom to buy a winning ticket. It'd solve all their financial worries in one go.

She yawned as she glanced down at the dots of gold still sitting on a plate on her desk. Hazel had exhausted herself just making those little things. What might attempting to create a real-life homunculus do?

And she remembered another of Van Stavern's warnings about the Crown—about using it on living creatures.

The results, Van Stavern had cautioned, were *disturbing*.

But Hazel's favorite book was *Frankenstein*. She was well aware of the horrific potential of playing god. In horror, the monsters you created rarely thanked you for the kindness.

Still, she emailed the article link about the homunculi to herself before closing the laptop. It didn't hurt to think about, right? And in the meantime, she still needed to sell her hard-won gold and earn enough money for a convention ticket.

Hazel heard her mom's bedroom door open just as she finished.

"Good morning!" Hazel called in a cheerful singsong, jumping up from her desk.

Considering her mom was about to head into yet another epic shift, the least Hazel could do was see her off with a smile. She'd already prepared a brown-bag lunch for her to take to work and brewed a pot of strong coffee to greet her as she roused. Even with employee discounts, the hospital cafeteria costs added up, so they made what they could at home.

Hazel grabbed the bag from the kitchen counter, turning toward the living room.

But when she found her mother standing with her phone in her hand—bleary-eyed and ashen-faced—Hazel's smile fell.

Her mom grabbed her suddenly by the shoulders, pulling Hazel into a fierce hug. Hazel dropped the lunch bag with a thud. She settled into the embrace, but her back remained stiff with dread. Something terrible had happened.

"Mom?" she said softly. "Mom, what's wrong?"

After a few moments, her mother finally rasped out an answer.

"They found Clara," she said. "She—she's gone."

"Gone . . ." Hazel echoed hollowly.

"I'm so sorry, honey," her mom said. "Clara's dead."

✕

"What do you mean, dead?" Serena asked, her voice leaden with shock. "What happened?'"

The three friends were back in the reliquary, each dressed in their pajamas. Hazel had called them all together as soon as her mom left for her shift.

"Mom didn't get into the details," Hazel said, "but I listened in on her phone conversation before she left. Something was wrong with the body. It sounded . . . like she was missing her heart."

Beside her, Emrys frowned. "That definitely seems paranormal."

"I remember Clara," Serena said. "Your old babysitter, right? She was the one who let us stay up late to watch *Walpurgis Night*, even though we were way too young."

Hazel nodded. She and Serena had both gotten nightmares from the film—an '80s slasher about a coven of killer witches who descended upon a suburban neighborhood. But Hazel cherished the memory. Clara was the first teenager who had treated Hazel like a mature young adult. It had been thrilling.

She could still see her mom's stricken face when she closed her eyes—the fear and grief she'd been too exhausted to conceal. What an awful thing . . .

"The police are supposedly investigating," Hazel said. "But we know at least some of them are involved with the Yellow Court. This has got to be a relic."

The Yellow Court. The secretive organization was yet another topic that Hazel knew frustratingly little about. According to Van Stavern, they had a collection of otherworldly relics all their own. But rather than keeping them safely away from the populace, the Yellow Court seemed to delight in dropping them into the middle of New Rotterdam, right where they'd do the most harm. Hazel couldn't begin to grasp why they'd want to hurt people.

"Any number of malignant entities are more than capable of extracting a heart," Van Stavern said. The Atlas was propped up on the table, its single eye swiveling across the room. "Some grim arcanists use them in dark rituals. Other creatures consume them, to gain their victims' strength or memories. Hearts are a very versatile ingredient, supernaturally speaking."

"How lucky for you that you lack one," Serena said pointedly. "So—where do we start investigating? I can search the wiki for clues, see if anything pops up."

"And I'll check the Atlas," Emrys chimed in. "With Van Stavern's help."

Hazel nodded. "Those are good starting places, but I think we should do some field research here—especially since we have the weekend. Clara disappeared during her shift at Grinning Gas. A jogger found her almost a mile away, near Centennial Park. Maybe if we search between those places, we'll learn something that can point us toward her killer."

"And what do we do if we *find* the killer?" Serena asked. She held up a hand as Emrys began to protest. "I'm not saying we don't go," she added quickly. "But the last time we hunted one of these things, it found us first. In the interest of not getting eaten alive again, I'd like to have a plan. Neither Hazel or I have even figured out how our relics work yet."

"That's . . . not entirely true," Hazel said, her face flushing.

Emrys turned to her with wide eyes. "You used the Crown? Hazel, that's amazing! Can I drink your first potion? What'd you make with it?"

Across the table, Van Stavern said nothing, but Hazel could feel the curiosity in the grimoire's stare. It made her self-conscious.

"Not much, honestly," she said. "I just switched some base metals around. It's a step, but a small one. And it won't protect us. For now, Emrys is still our only firepower. His *weird spell*—"

"Weirdlight," Emrys said. He smiled shyly, sinking into his chair. "That's what I'm calling the hex."

Hazel nodded. She'd missed the first explosive application of the spell, when Emrys used it to save himself and Serena from Edna Milton. But she'd seen plenty of practice shots since then. The hex's destructive potential was alarming, truth be told. Thankfully, Emrys was on their side.

"The *weirdlight* will have to do, until we can all figure out how to weaponize our relics."

"Fine," Serena said with a sigh. "But I'm bringing my brother's bear spray. Hopefully it works just as well on monsters."

Hazel yawned. "I still need to shower and run a quick errand. Let's meet out front around noon?"

"Sure, but . . ." Serena paused, biting her lip.

"What is it?" Hazel asked. She could hear the impatience creeping into her tone, but she still had to get to the pawnshop and back.

"Don't take this the wrong way," Serena said, "but maybe you should sleep in a bit more. You look pale. Self-care is important, too, you know."

Hazel bit back the scoff that wanted to burst from her apparently pale lips. *Self-care?* It was the sort of phrase that rich people bandied about. They couldn't even perceive how expensive leisure truly was.

"I'm fine," she replied, simply and tersely.

Serena raised her hands and shrugged. "Okay."

Though she could feel exhaustion tugging at her already, Hazel didn't have time to spare. If the police really were investigating Clara's death—or more likely, covering the killer's tracks for the Yellow Court—then every moment might count.

And, more selfishly, if Hazel wanted to attend RotterCon with her friends, then she needed to get to work turning her handful of gold into a wallet full of cash.

"I have some good news, though," she ventured as she stood. The mood had darkened in the reliquary, and Hazel understood that it was her doing, rather than some cursed artifact's. Perhaps a bit of positivity was in order. "I think I'm making headway with my mom about RotterCon. I should know for sure when we meet up later."

"Hey, that's great!" Emrys said. "It really wouldn't be the same without you."

I can do it all, Hazel thought to herself. *I've got this under control.*

If magic wanted to tell a story, Hazel was determined hers would have a happy ending.

4

Bullion Buyers wasn't far from the laundromat where Hazel had washed her mom's scrubs just last night, but she still nearly missed the derelict little shop. It was tucked off the main road, sandwiched between an abandoned construction site and a severe brick building that Hazel couldn't begin to guess the purpose of.

The shop's sign was sun bleached nearly to illegibility, which was quite a feat in a town where the sun rarely deigned to visit. Most of the blocky print was ghostly pale, with only the letters *L*, *I*, *E*, and *S* still retaining some of their red coloring.

An electronic bell pinged as Hazel opened the front door, though no one was waiting behind the counter. The shop was lit by harsh fluorescent tubes overhead, though the first thing she noticed was all the glass. The entire space was lined in transparent panes—display cases and cabinets and rotating containers—all of them packed full of shiny metal trinkets. And each was sealed behind an enormous steel lock, some as large as Hazel's fist.

She heard a groan emanate from behind a flimsy particle-board door leading to a back office. The voice did not sound pleased to be roused.

Hazel caught the tail end of a muttered litany as a figure emerged.

". . . ungodly hour," the man finished, before his eyes settled on her. Then his eyebrows shot up. "A kid?" he said. "Shouldn't you be in school?"

"It's Saturday," Hazel answered in a small voice.

"What's your point?"

The man wore a soiled polo shirt, and his face was lined in patchy stubble that looked a few days old. His white skin was pocked and veiny. Hazel suspected the fluorescent lighting wasn't doing either of them any favors that morning.

Nearly every part of her wanted to turn right there and exit the shop. Facing this cantankerous grown-up in her exhausted state was more daunting than actual alchemy had been. But she'd come this far. She couldn't give up now.

"You . . . you buy gold, right?" Hazel asked. Usually she was so good with adults, but the strangeness of this situation—combined with her bone-deep weariness—had her feeling off-balance. "I want to sell some."

The man eyed her suspiciously. "Kid, this isn't the playground. We do real business here."

"That's good," Hazel said. "Because I have real gold. Twenty-four karats." She knew that karats were the measure of purity for gold alloys, with twenty-four representing the purest and most valuable.

The man crossed his arms and frowned, but after a moment he simply grunted, "Let's see what you've got."

Hazel approached the glass counter, where the man set out a large metal tray. He nodded toward it. Hazel retrieved the glittering beads from her pocket, dropping them into the tray with a clatter. They looked so small in the expansive plate.

The gold buyer must have thought so, too. He coughed out a laugh that smelled strongly of burned coffee.

"Oh man," he said, sliding his hand over his unshaven face. "This is not how I expected my morning to go. Listen, ki—"

"Hazel," said Hazel. "My name isn't kid."

The shopkeeper shrugged. "Listen, *Hazel*. Usually when people invest in gold, it's in coins or bars. Even if I bought scrap gold at this shop—which I don't, unless you represent a legitimate business like a jewelry manufacturer—this wouldn't be enough to be worth my time. We're talking wholesale."

Hazel felt her throat tightening in disappointment. How had she been so stupid? Of course it wouldn't be this easy.

"Please," she said. "Maybe you could make an exception just this once? I need the money. And I can get more gold if you'll buy these now—enough to make it worthwhile."

The shopkeeper's eyes narrowed.

"Where exactly did you find these?" he asked. He picked up one of the beads, gazing closely at it. "They don't look like dental fillings or jewelry . . . Did you steal them?"

"What?" Hazel said. "No!"

"Then where'd they come from?" the man asked. His tone was suddenly light, even conversational. It sent a shiver of fear through Hazel. Rather than setting the bead back down in the tray, he picked up the others, cradling the droplets in his palm.

Hazel didn't have a good answer for him. What could she even say? She couldn't claim she'd found them, now that she'd promised more. But she also couldn't very well reveal that she'd made the gold. She needed to get out of there. To regroup and rethink her plan, hopefully when she was less tired.

"I . . . I'd like my gold back now, please," Hazel said. "If you're not going to buy it from me."

The man crossed his arms again, leaning back against the discolored wall behind the counter. "Well, you still haven't answered my question, though," he said. "And that's giving me a whole bunch of *other* questions. Like what exactly a kid might need quick cash for. And why they'd try selling a bunch of scrap gold without their mommy or daddy present." He tapped his chin thoughtfully. "I bet the police might be really curious about some of those questions, too, huh?"

It was like the floor had suddenly given out beneath her. Was this guy seriously threatening to call the cops? Hazel had come there in secret. She hadn't told her mom, or even Serena and Emrys, what she was planning. Now she risked thrusting the NRPD into their lives, a development that would be complicating at best and catastrophic at worst.

"Please . . ." Hazel rasped. "Don't." She hated the sound of helplessness in her own voice. How had this spun out of control so quickly?

"Tell you what, *Hazel*," the shopkeeper said. "Let's make a deal after all. You turn around and walk out that door right now, and we'll pretend this never happened. I'll finish my coffee and forget all my questions, and you can go watch cartoons. Do normal kid stuff."

"But . . . my . . . ?"

The man smiled, still holding Hazel's gold beads in his palm.

So that was his game. He was really going to steal from a *child*. And Hazel didn't have any choice but to let him. With the NRPD already infiltrated by the Yellow Court, she couldn't afford drawing their attention, especially if she and her friends planned to investigate Clara's death.

Hazel's eyes burned with frustration. It was all so unfair. She'd done everything right. She'd researched and planned and even coaxed an ancient, magical relic to do the impossible. She'd fed her own essence or energy or whatever to the Magnus Crown to create those golden beads, and now this awful man was going to snatch them away with a smile.

She wished she could transmute this feeling into something useful. Something *powerful*. But the Crown didn't work like that. Against the selfishness and indifference of grown-ups, it was about as useful as a tin paperweight.

So instead, Hazel did the only thing she could.

She left the shop without another word.

✕

It was easy to spot the glossy yellow police tape against the greens and grays of Centennial Park. It stretched from tree to tree, marking a small grassy area as off-limits. Weekend parkgoers gave the area a wide berth—and sometimes a quick, curious peek—as they went about their leisure.

Hazel and her friends edged closer. She'd been in a foul mood when they'd reconvened in front of the apartment building. Thankfully, Emrys and Serena seemed to sense her displeasure. Neither asked about the convention, instead giving her space to fume and keeping their conversations to the task at hand. Hazel was grateful for that, at least.

As they stepped off the dirt trail and beneath the thick-grown canopy, the bright day darkened, taking on a twilight quality. Hazel was reminded of fairy tales where the hero was warned against straying from the path.

"I forgot this place was even here," said Emrys. "It's so strange. Like this little bit of nature was protected somehow as the city grew up all around it."

"There's a story about that," Hazel said. "A vengeful wood nymph or something." She shook her head. "But it isn't true. This whole park was designed and built by architects."

"What, really?" Emrys rapped his knuckles on the nearest tree as if expecting to find it hollow.

"Really," said Hazel. "That tree is a European hornbeam. It's not native to this hemisphere. I think they even brought the *rocks* in from some quarry somewhere. The architects had to fight city hall to make it happen, but they argued that without access to green spaces, the people of New Rotterdam would go mad."

Serena sniffed. "Maybe they should have built a bigger park."

"Hold up," Emrys whispered, and he grabbed each of them by the wrist, stopping their slow march through the trees. He ducked low, pulling them down with him. Hazel stifled a complaint at the rough handling; she knew Emrys well enough to know when he was genuinely spooked.

Up ahead, near the police tape, there was the sound of crunching leaves. As Hazel watched, a figure came into view, stepping out from behind a thick ash tree. He was tall, almost unnaturally so, with pallid skin and thin, bloodless lips. Hazel recognized him immediately as a cop; she'd seen him at her school during the Wandering Hour case.

And she'd seen him with Mayor Royce on the TV, the night they realized the mayor was connected to the Yellow Court.

It had been such a small clue—a golden chess piece worn as a pin on his lapel during a TV interview. But that evidence, coupled with a jolt to their spooky senses that even Hazel had felt acutely, was enough to convince the friends that Royce and those detectives were in league with the Order's greatest enemies.

The man stood staring listlessly into space, arms across his chest, swaying like a cobra. After a moment, he spit onto the ground, then shuffled back the way he'd come. It looked to Hazel as if he were guarding the crime scene; if they'd come any closer, he would have spotted them for certain.

Emrys tugged on them, urging them to go back the way they'd come. Hazel followed his lead, stepping as lightly as possible through the brush.

"That was close," Emrys said. "We should avoid that guy if we can. Him and his partner."

Partner. At the reminder, Hazel scanned their surroundings.

"A sound plan," Van Stavern said, muffled slightly by the tote in which Emrys carried him. "The Yellow Court are insidious and startlingly widespread. And, as we've learned, capable of a great many horrors."

Hazel felt a buzzing in her skull. It was so faint, she almost missed it. She closed her eyes and focused on the feeling. It felt almost directional, like a compass, and when she opened her eyes, she was looking directly at the second cop. He was squat, toad-like, sitting absolutely still on a bench farther up the path. He hadn't spotted them. Yet.

"Let's keep moving," Hazel said. Then, lowering her voice: "The other one is right over there. *Don't* look."

"Did he see us?" Emrys asked, dutifully resisting any urge he felt to look over his shoulder.

"I don't know," Hazel answered. "I don't think so."

"I'll map the most direct route to the gas station where Clara worked," Serena said. "Keep your eyes peeled."

"If I may?" Van Stavern interjected. Emrys made sure none of the joggers or dog walkers were too close, then he hefted the book from his tote. "This park was the gathering site for a particularly pernicious cult in the eighties. I don't like to brag, but I had a *not insignificant* role in taking them down. Perhaps a version of the story is documented in your wiki?"

"I could check," Serena offered brightly. "Was this in the early 1880s or later on?"

"It was the *1980s*, thank you very much!" the book growled. "You all know I'm not that old, don't you?"

Hazel caught Serena's satisfied smirk. She'd definitely done that on purpose.

"So you think the cult's back?" Emrys asked.

"I wonder if we can get our hands on the autopsy report," Hazel said. "Cultists with a knife would leave a very different type of wound than a monster. Or than a human with relic-enhanced powers, even."

"You're scarily good at this," Serena said flatly.

Hazel shrugged. "Everything has rules," she said. "Even magic. They might not be the same rules we're used to, but that doesn't mean we can't learn to control them."

"A reasonable expectation," Van Stavern said, "which is precisely what makes it so wrong."

Hazel bristled, frowning at the Atlas's leathery eye.

"Where the relics' powers touch our world, the rules erode," Van Stavern continued. "They *warp*. You must always expect the unexpected, even of your own growing powers. An urge for control and rationality can put one directly at odds with the unseen world. Remember: it is the hand that grips most tightly to the reins that suffers injury when those reins are yanked away."

Hazel groaned. Van Stavern wasn't making any sense!

"Then what? Should we just give up?" She wheeled around to face the book. "How are we supposed to fight these things without understanding them? How do we use our relics without *controlling* them? And I swear, if you spout some nonsense about telling a story—"

"Hazel, hey," Serena said, putting a hand on her shoulder. "It's okay." Still, she loyally shot Van Stavern a withering glare.

"No, it isn't," Hazel said, shaking her head. But she took a deep breath. "Sorry. It's been a long couple days. And Clara . . . Clara didn't deserve this."

"No," Van Stavern answered, an uncharacteristic melancholy in his tone. "None of you do. And it's natural to try and make sense of the senseless. But you yourself said that assumptions can distort our observations. I merely mean that you should conduct your investigations with an open mind. Rigid ones tend to be the first to . . . break."

Hazel didn't care for the book's lecture. Yes, she had an orderly and analytical mind, but she was hardly a *skeptic*. After all, she'd believed in some version of the unseen world long before they'd stumbled upon the proof contained within the Doomsday Archives. She'd somehow known all along that the unseen world was all around them. If she didn't grip the reins—if she didn't guide her friends past the gnashing teeth to safety—then who would?

There was a small crowd up ahead, and Hazel suddenly realized where the path had led them. They were approaching the park's most infamous landmark.

"The Faceless Founder," said Emrys, with a little bit of awe in his voice.

The allegedly murderous statue was also a social media darling. Tourists were clustered around its base, taking selfies.

For just a second, Hazel considered whether the statue could be the killer. Were all the old stories true? Except what use did a cursed statue have for a heart? It was supposed to be after faces, for obvious reasons.

"I don't feel anything," Emrys said, a pang of sadness in his voice.

"That's because you live here now, dear child," said Serena. "Only out-of-towners get the ooky-spookies from the local eyesores."

"But we should get the spookies if there's anything supernatural nearby. Right?" Emrys pointed to his eye. "I'm not getting any tingles."

Hazel realized he was right. "Me neither."

Emrys turned to her. "Does that mean the statue is just . . . a statue?"

"I-I don't know . . ." Hazel hesitated. "We don't really understand how our spooky sense works. So until we know more, we probably shouldn't rely on it too heavily. What if a relic can't be sensed when it's dormant or camouflaged? We could be tricked, trapped . . . lulled into thinking we're safe when we're not."

Despite her annoyance, Hazel was a bit unnerved by Van Stavern's warning. If there truly were no rules where the unseen world was concerned, then what *could* she trust? Nothing. It was a deeply unsettling thought.

The city awaited them just past the edge of the park. There was no gradual transition to ease them back into the urban landscape. The dirt path suddenly became a sidewalk; the trees were replaced with streetlamps, and the sounds of traffic overtook the birdsong. Still, it was an unusually bright day in New Rotterdam. If they were meant to be looking for anything out of the ordinary, the only thing that fit the bill was the absence of the city's ubiquitous fog, which had seemingly burned away in the sunlight. The sidewalks were crowded, buzzing with a carnival atmosphere. The people of New Rotterdam knew to make the most of a sunny Saturday.

To Hazel's mind, it only made Clara's death more tragic. As if the sun itself had decided the girl wouldn't be mourned.

Even the gas station where she'd worked was open for business. There was none of the crime scene tape they'd seen at the park. It was a small station, with only two gas pumps out front and three narrow parking spots. The interior was likewise cramped, a lone aisle forced to play host to an unlikely assortment of junk food, cleaning materials, and automotive supplies. It was a mess, but not in the way that indicated a struggle had taken place. Hazel worried that their investigation had reached a dead end.

Serena had other ideas. She walked up to the counter, where a teenage boy with severe bangs and a lip ring tapped idly on his phone. "Can I help you?" he asked without looking up from his screen.

"I hope so," said Serena. "I wanted to ask you some questions about Clara."

Now he looked up, eyes narrowed in suspicion. "What kind of questions?"

"We want to find out what happened to her. We're . . ." Serena cast about for a halfway plausible lie. "We're with the school newspaper."

"Which school?"

"Sacred Silence," answered Serena, at the exact moment Emrys said, "Gideon."

The boy—his name tag said *Byron*—raised an eyebrow.

"Byron," Hazel tried. "I'm Hazel. My friends and I are sorry about what happened to Clara, and the truth is, we just want to make sure that it doesn't happen to anyone else."

"Yeah, Byron," Serena added, and she pulled out a twenty-dollar bill. "Maybe we can help each other out." She dropped it into a brightly decorated tip jar on the counter, which read COLLEGE FUND! in big, blocky letters.

Hazel gasped. That had been the fastest she'd ever seen anyone toss away twenty dollars. That was *half* a ticket to RotterCon. "Serena!"

"What? It's for a good cause," Serena said. "College, right?"

The boy smirked, some of his hostility falling away. "That's not *exactly* true. The jar was Clara's idea, actually. She said we'd get more tips if people thought it was for college. But I'm saving up for a gaming laptop, and she was trying to buy a car. It's all she talked about."

"So you knew her pretty well?" asked Emrys.

"Not well, but our shifts overlapped," said the boy. "She'd be on the way out when I was on my way in. She'd even cover for me and stick around if I was ever running late." He shrugged. "That's how I knew something was wrong yesterday. When I got here—a few minutes early, for once—the place was empty. Then the police showed up."

"You called the police right away?" asked Serena.

"No, it's weird, actually." Byron frowned. "They just showed up. Said the silent alarm had been tripped. I obviously took the opportunity to tell them I was worried about Clara. They said they'd look for her, but . . . I guess that jogger beat them to it."

"Did the police find anything here?" Hazel asked. "Did they look for clues?"

"They wanted the video footage," Byron answered. At Hazel's questioning look, he added, "The footage from the security camera just outside. They said it might help them find her, so I handed it over, obviously."

"Do you have a spare copy?" Hazel asked.

"No. They took the only tape . . ."

"Darn it," said Serena.

". . . from the *exterior* camera." The boy pointed at the far corner of the ceiling. "But we've got a camera *inside*, too. They didn't ask about it, and I didn't offer." He grinned. "I'll sell it to you for a hundred bucks."

"A hundred bucks!" echoed Hazel. "But . . . we're trying to solve a murder. To *help* people."

"So help *me*," said Byron.

"To buy a laptop?"

The boy leveled her with a serious look. "Don't judge me," he said. "Believe me, you don't end up a cashier in a place like this if you don't need money bad."

"What's on the recording?" asked Emrys.

"Don't know," said the boy. "Haven't watched it."

"Fifty bucks," Serena countered.

"Seventy-five," said the boy.

"Fifty," Serena repeated. "And you throw in a thing of Oreos."

"Deal." The boy held out his hand, and Serena counted out the cash. Hazel tried to keep her face calm as she watched. All told, Serena had just spent nearly double what a convention ticket cost, as if it were nothing. Hazel thought back to her own miserable exchange with the gold buyer that morning.

It was almost comical. She couldn't trade real gold for forty measly dollars, and yet this Byron had made *seventy* on the promise of a video.

Of course, Hazel realized she could just ask Serena for the money. Her friend would happily give it to her. Yet Hazel's mind went immediately to the faux-leather backpack buried in her closet. She'd kept her family's financial troubles a secret for so long. She wasn't sure she knew how to talk about them, or how such a revelation might change things between her and her friends.

No. Better to handle her problems herself. Van Stavern was wrong. When the reins were being yanked away, that wasn't when you handed them over to someone else. That was the moment you held on for dear life.

Satisfied, Byron retrieved a VHS tape from under the counter and slid it over to Serena.

"Wait, it's an actual *tape?*" Serena's surprise was obvious. "How are we supposed to watch this thing?"

Byron shrugged. "Not my problem. Although I could let you use our playback equipment for, oh, another fifty bucks . . ."

"Forget it," Serena said, and she handed the tape over to Hazel. "We'll manage. Emrys, grab some cookies."

"Oh, shoot," said Hazel, as she slipped the VHS tape into her satchel. "I forgot I've got my mom's lunch in here." She looked up at her friends. "With everything that happened this morning, she forgot to take it to work." She checked the time on her phone. "If I hurry, I can still get it to her before her break."

"We'll come with you," Emrys offered. "Maybe they've got a VCR in the break room."

"Maybe," agreed Hazel. "Although the new wing is supposed to be totally state of the art, since that billionaire donated all that money. I still haven't seen it from the inside."

"Let's go," Serena said, sparing one last dirty look for Byron. Hazel was so distracted that as she pushed open the door, she nearly slammed it into the person standing just outside.

"Oh, sorry, I—" she said, and then she stopped short.

It was the cop. The tall one they'd seen in the park.

He looked down at her, and his thin lips parted in an eerie, predatory smile.

Captain Kazoo's Journeys Through the 4th Dimension

From the New Rotterdam Wiki Project

Among the more difficult New Rotterdam legends to verify is a long-running but obscure television show titled *Captain Kazoo's Journeys Through the 4th Dimension*, which has supposedly aired on local channel WROT-13 since the 1970s. While many New Rotterdam locals can recall watching the show as children—often in the dark hours of morning before their parents awoke—no recording of it has ever been produced.

In a 1995 interview with Melinda Freese, then president of WROT-13, a reporter for the New Rotterdam Watcher discussed the mysterious broadcast, including his own memories of the sometimes disturbing content. Freese adamantly denied that such a program had ever existed, much less had been airing from the station for two decades without her knowledge.

Indeed, no proof has ever materialized supporting the show's existence. It never appeared on any programming schedules, and no studio has come forward claiming credit for producing it. Still, local residents can recount in vivid detail its characters, plots, and occasionally menacing tone.

According to witness accounts, the show centered on a hapless astronaut named Captain Kazoo and his crew of bizarre and fanciful creatures in their journeys through the cosmos. Kazoo's spaceship, the *NRS Unspeakable*, could travel vast distances through what he cheerfully dubbed "the 4th dimension," a psychedelic parallel universe where immense and unsettling shadows watched from a distance. Trips through the 4th dimension were frequently remembered with dread by viewers, who noted odd whispers in the background audio and stars that took on shapes reminiscent of mouths full of glittering teeth.

There is one notable piece of evidence supporting the show's existence. In 1992, ten-year-old Jeremy Waller—who claimed to be a fan of the program—discovered a Captain Kazoo toy prize in his Cosmic Krispies breakfast cereal one morning. Indeed, the action figure Jeremy shared with the *New Rotterdam Watcher* resembled the character described by viewers: a smiling astronaut clutching a dark and pitted stone that was warm to the touch. Most believed the toy was an elaborate hoax, but when the *Watcher* reporter had samples of the stone sent for examination, he was surprised to discover it was in fact a meteorite, one verified to have come from the 1940 Meteor Shower.[1]

References

1. MacDonald, Kip (31 October 1992). "Local 'Space Cadet' Claims Breakfast Toy Is 'Constellation Prize.'" *New Rotterdam Watcher.*

5

"Hello, children."

The police officer's greeting was as sharp and surprising as a stranger pushing against the front door. Hazel froze at the sound of it, dread setting her fingers tingling. She unconsciously hugged her satchel closer. Within it was the secret tape of the gas station's interior footage.

"Officer," Serena said smoothly behind her, "please excuse us."

But the cop didn't move. His tall, wiry frame still blocked them in. Hazel took a step back, making room for him to enter and hopefully move past them. The man stepped in but strode no farther.

"It's *detective*, actually," the man said, his eyes never leaving Hazel's. "Detective Pryce. You look familiar, kid. Don't suppose I've had to bring you in?" Detective Pryce smiled, but there wasn't a hint of friendliness in it. His thin teeth looked unsettlingly sharp.

Serena scoffed. "You're more likely to have arrested the Easter Bunny," she said. "This girl *doesn't* get in trouble."

Again, Hazel thought back to the gold buyer's threat of calling the cops. She felt her face heating.

"That so?" The man's head tilted, but his body stayed oddly still. "Then I don't suppose you know anything about the violent crime that happened here last night?" Pryce's large, expressive eyes were bright—almost raving. "A girl was murdered."

Why did he look *excited*?

Hazel glanced toward Byron behind the counter, but the young cashier seemed to have disappeared. It was as good a time as any to do inventory.

"That's terrible," Hazel said noncommittally. She turned back to the man. "Do you have any suspects?"

"Oh, we'll find someone," said Pryce. "A drifter. A transient. Some freak."

Hazel stiffened. She could practically feel Emrys and Serena doing the same behind her. Every teacher and grown-up they'd ever met told them not to use words like that, but here was a *police detective* throwing it around.

"Though sometimes," the man continued, "it's the ones you don't expect. Like family . . . or even friends." Pryce swayed on his feet, his wide eyes intensely focused. "Hey—you didn't know the victim, did you? Clara?"

Hazel panicked. Clara had babysat Hazel when she was younger. She'd been in Hazel's *home*. Was that suspicious?

They'd also just pressed Byron for details about Clara's disappearance. If the detective questioned him, what would he say? Would he tell them about the tape?

Hazel had only barely avoided drawing the police's attention that morning, but now she'd walked right into their path. Exhaustion pulled at her from all sides, fraying her thoughts. Just like at Bullion Buyers, she couldn't seem to come up with a good answer. And the longer she stood there, gawping in silence, the more suspicious she looked. She could feel herself spiraling.

But this time Hazel wasn't alone. Serena came to her rescue. "High schoolers don't generally hang out with sixth graders," she said, brilliantly evading the question. "Now, if you don't mind, we've got teeth to rot." She held up the pack of Oreos.

"Sure, sure," Detective Pryce said, showing off his own disturbing smile. "Hey, if you hear or see anything strange—anything connected to Clara—give us a call, okay?"

He flicked a business card from the pocket of his dark suit jacket, holding it out for Hazel to take. Pryce stood perfectly still, his grin frozen in anticipation. His hand was just far enough away that Hazel would have to step forward to retrieve the card.

She hesitated, but after a beat, forced herself to move, reaching nervously to pluck it from his waiting hand.

And the moment her fingertips brushed against it, her spooky sense exploded.

Hazel nearly cried out in surprise. The sudden pressure behind her eye was debilitating, almost painful in its fervency. But she could feel Pryce's eyes studying her, waiting for a reaction.

This was a trap. Somehow, the detective had weaponized her spooky sense against her. Hazel hadn't felt *anything* a moment ago—now her sixth sense was on fire.

Who . . . or what . . . was this man?

Thankfully for Hazel, years of practice pushing down her feelings kicked immediately into gear. She swallowed her surprise, ignoring the tears welling behind her eye, and took the card into her palm. Hazel quickly tucked it into the satchel beside the VHS tape.

"We will, Officer," she rasped, stepping back beside her friends. "*Detective*, I mean."

Detective Pryce nodded slowly, his eyes searching her face. Then, with a jerky movement made all the more sudden by his previous stillness, he stepped out of the way of the door.

Hazel hurried past. Her right eye was blazing. Tears would begin falling soon enough, which not even the best poker face could hide. She heard Emrys and Serena hustling behind her, but Hazel kept moving. She wanted to put as much distance between her and that awful man as she could.

But as she crossed the parking lot, Hazel felt it again. Her spooky sense fluttered, and there was the other, squatter detective, watching her go from the nearby bench. The man barely moved, except to drink from an enormous jug of water he carried at his side. He lifted the heavy thing unhurriedly to his lips, guzzling from the spout in slow, ponderous swallows. When he lowered it, little trails of moisture still lingered in the corners of his mouth.

Hazel walked as fast as she dared. Tears were now dripping freely from her right eye. She swiped quickly at her face with the back of her hand, moving in the direction of the hospital.

"What happened back there?" Emrys said, once Hazel had finally responded to his and Serena's pleas to slow down.

They were three blocks away from the gas station before the buzz finally settled, and even then, Hazel's still-jangling nerves screamed at her to move. It took all her willpower to plant her feet long enough for her friends to catch up.

"You didn't *feel* that?" she said, wheeling on the two.

"I felt something," Serena said. "When we were outside."

Emrys nodded in agreement.

"But not in the gas station? Not from Detective Pryce?"

Serena and Emrys looked at one another and then back at Hazel expectantly.

She shivered. "The moment I touched the card . . . God, it was nearly as bad as the night we found the reliquary."

"But I didn't feel anything," Emrys said worriedly.

"I think that was the point," Hazel replied. "It was like Detective Pryce was waiting until the moment I got close to set off my senses all at once. Like he was prodding me to see if I'd react."

"How is that possible?" Serena said. "Hey, book guy— explain."

Emrys pulled the composition notebook from his bag. A moment later, Van Stavern's leathery eye swiveled on the three.

"It is *possible* that some particularly pernicious entities could disguise themselves from our sight. But I've never heard of them using our sixth sense against us in such a fashion. This is . . . a disturbing development."

"And it's *exactly* why we need to learn the rules for this stuff!" Hazel fumed. "Pryce took me by surprise in there. Who knows what would have happened if I'd broken down in front of him?"

"Hey," Emrys said pacifyingly. "But you did great, Hazel. Everything worked out."

"*This* time!"

"Test and experiment all you like," Van Stavern said. "I'm afraid it won't shield you from unpleasant surprises. That is not how this works."

Hazel wanted to scream. She hated feeling out of control, hated not knowing how *this worked*. Back when she and Emrys were just obsessed with the wiki, understanding had been a click away. All the information she needed on her town's supernatural otherworld was right there in lines of clean black text, citations at the ready.

But Van Stavern's arrival had changed all that. Suddenly the wiki was just the tip of the eerie iceberg. There were things swimming in those depths that Hazel couldn't begin to comprehend, much less combat.

She turned, gazing into the distance, where Saint Azazel Hospital's clean architecture and shiny green windows rose up to meet a rare blue sky. Hazel found the sight comforting. It stilled her nerves. Hospitals were places where knowledge prevailed, or at least where bodies acted according to certain rules.

And her mom was in there.

"Let's just go," she said. "We still need to find a way to watch this tape."

"Hold on." Serena reached into Hazel's satchel, frowning as her fingers grasped for something. Finally, she pulled out the business card Pryce had given them. She turned the card so Hazel and Emrys could see the front. It was plain white cardstock, with the badge symbol for the NRPD emblazoned on the left.

But there, under the name Detective Reginald Pryce, was another symbol—a small, decorative flourish that was strangely out of place.

It was a yellow chess piece, shaped like a knight.

"I don't know about you two," Serena said wearily, "but I'm really starting to hate that game."

The Possession of Emmet Grove 🔒

From the New Rotterdam Wiki Project

Fred and Lottie Weeble were paranormal investigators who operated in New Rotterdam from the 1950s through 1992. Fred was a self-described "supernaturist" and exorcist, while Lottie claimed to be a scent medium who could communicate with spirits through smell. Together, the two founded the New Rotterdam Psychic Development Response Partnership (NeRPDeRP), one of many ghost-hunting groups to spring up in the region at the time.

Though the pair struggled in the early years to convince prospective clients that their homes were haunted and in need of expensive cleansing rituals, one case brought with it a degree of notoriety that set off their rise to prominence.

In 1958, Emmet Grove discovered a strange lantern hidden behind a brick wall in his family's basement. The lantern housed a candle whose melted wax resembled a screaming human face. Upon lighting the candle, Emmet immediately fell into a catatonic state. When his parents couldn't wake him, they called on the Weebles for help. The paranormal investigators concluded that Emmet had been possessed by a malevolent

spirit residing within the candle, and only by conducting a dangerous and costly exorcism would the boy be released.

Fred worked for three days without success, while Lottie smelled around the basement for hints of the spirit's nature and weaknesses. Then, just as the Groves were losing hope and patience, a stranger appeared at their door on the morning of the fourth day, claiming to be an "archivist" associated with "the Order." Assuming he worked with the Weebles, the Groves let the archivist into Emmet's bedroom. But when the Weebles arrived later that morning, they claimed no knowledge of the man.

Rushing to Emmet's room, the families found the boy sitting up in bed, awake and alert. There was no sign of the archivist nor the mysterious lantern. When asked where the man had gone, Emmet nodded toward his closet, saying simply, "Watch the doors."

The Weebles were quick to claim responsibility for Emmet's miraculous recovery, alleging that the "archivist" was a manifestation of the offending evil spirit, finally banished through their work. Word of the boy's revival spread quickly throughout the city, catapulting the duo to fame.

See also

The Weebles' Museum of Sinister Stuff
Headless Kate
A Haunting Odor

6

They knew they were nearing the hospital by the sound of the sirens.

Saint Azazel Hospital was massive and labyrinthine—a complex of interlocking buildings connected by glass-enclosed skywalks and underground walkways. To Hazel, the place looked a bit like a bad game of Tetris—mismatched shapes set down at random with too much negative space between them.

There was a reason for the chaos. Saint Azazel was nearly as old as New Rotterdam itself, and as the city had grown, so too had its premier hospital. But the old buildings couldn't be demolished to make way for new construction—where would the patients go?—and so expansions, extensions, and entirely new buildings had been added to the hospital as the centuries had progressed. The Worthmann Pediatric Center, opened only a year ago, was sleek and modern and bore the name of the wealthy philanthropist who'd funded its construction.

Hazel's mom worked in the oldest building, nearly lost in the shadow of the new tower. Its white stone columns and faded brick facade marked it as unmistakably colonial.

The architecture didn't appear to be making an impression on Emrys. He was too busy plugging his ears.

"That siren is so loud!" he complained. "Why isn't it *moving?*"

Hazel, gritting her teeth against the noise, turned to look into the street. Ambulances were always coming and going from the hospital complex, sent out into the city like drone insects from their hive.

Except insects didn't have to worry about inner-city gridlock.

The ambulance's shrill siren underscored the urgency of its mission, but there was no way through the traffic—nowhere for all the cars on the narrow road to go. The ambulance was forced to wait, just like everybody else.

Hazel hoped that whoever needed that ambulance could hold on a little longer. Traffic in New Rotterdam really could be killer.

✕

Despite knowing the guard on duty, Hazel couldn't get her friends through security.

"No ID, no admittance," he said with a shrug.

Hazel fought a swell of frustration. This was the pawnshop all over again; an adult throwing his authority around, telling her no when he could just as easily say *yes*. In a game of Dungeons & Dragons, she would simply make a charisma check with the roll of a die. In real life, it was up to her to come up with the right argument.

She eyed the metal detector, which had been installed a few years ago and still seemed out of place in the centuries-old lobby. "You're not worried about a couple of kids hurting anybody?" she prompted.

"We live in strange times, Miss Hazel," said the guard, and he shook his head sadly. "Liability, you understand. Rules are rules. Without their parents here . . ."

As he spoke, a kid around their age walked past, waving to the guard as she stepped through the metal detector and deeper into the building.

"What about her?" she asked. "I didn't see her parents."

"Student volunteer," said the guard. He swept his eyes over Emrys and Serena. "Hospital's always looking for more, actually, if you've got time on your hands."

"We'll . . . think about it," Emrys said. Hazel could already tell he was one of those people who felt on edge in a hospital.

Serena pulled Hazel from the desk. "Hazel, it's fine, really. Visit your mom. Emrys and I will head home and ask around the building for a VCR. One of our neighbors is bound to have one."

"Good idea," confirmed Emrys.

"Yeah, okay," said Hazel, and she handed over the tape, a bit reluctantly. She remembered the last time she'd split off from the two of them. "Just don't solve the whole thing without me this time, all right?"

×

Hazel's mom was with a patient, so Hazel waited by the nurses' station, taking a seat and tapping at her phone screen. She didn't actually have anything to look at—no new notifications, and she'd already done her daily quests in Yeti Sanctuary—but her mind was restless, and she didn't want to be in anybody's way.

She was also actively trying not to eavesdrop, but it was hard not to listen. The nurses at the station were speaking in low, conspiratorial voices. Hazel naturally assumed they'd be talking about Clara, but the name she heard instead was Julius Worthmann. The philanthropist seemed to have plans for this wing of the hospital, too.

"Did you hear how disruptive the construction was in the children's wing?" said one nurse. "Imagine a rich man dropping in for a photo op every five minutes, and you're just here trying to do your job."

"You can't argue with the results, though," said another. "Have you been over there? The man's got taste, and it shows, from the wallpaper to the windows."

"We don't need the hospital to look nice on Snappygram," countered the first nurse. "We need to hire more people and to buy more equipment. He wants to give us money? Great, but let us decide how to spend it."

At last, Hazel heard her mom's voice around the corner. "Dr. Strathmore, I've barely seen my daughter in weeks. I'm a single mother and I have the time off. I need to be able to use it."

Hazel's heart fell. Her mom's desperate tone was almost more than she could bear. Her mom was running on fumes, and it was all because of *Hazel*.

"Lisa, I understand. I do. And if Worthmann really does decide to fund the wing, I'll be first in line demanding we allocate money for more staff. But Ginny's daughter is dead. We can't tell her to come in."

"I don't know how much longer I can do this," Hazel's mom said.

"Please," the other voice—Dr. Strathmore—replied. "Stay with us until we can get Worthmann on board. I *know* we're close. If I have to beg, I will. I'm not above it."

Hazel peered around the corner. Down the hallway, her mom was having a conversation with a man Hazel had met a handful of times. He wore a stethoscope around his neck and a pleading expression on his face.

Hazel's mom took a deep breath. "All right," she said. "I'm sorry. Honestly, I'm just so tired. I know I'm being insensitive, but after what happened to Clara, I can't help worrying about Hazel, all alone."

"Don't apologize," Dr. Strathmore said. "We're all being stretched thin these days."

"This must be hard on you, too," Hazel's mom said, rubbing her face. "How's your sister?"

"No progress yet," the doctor said, a sad smile not quite masking his discomfort. "But I'm still hopeful."

"Well, she's lucky to have you looking after her. If anyone can break through, it's you."

Hazel quickly realized this was not a conversation she wanted to be a part of. Her mom hadn't seen her yet; she ducked into the nearest open room.

It was occupied.

"Oh!" she said. "Sorry, I didn't mean to barge in."

A girl looked up—the volunteer she'd seen come through the lobby. She had light brown skin and about a million piercings.

"No worries," said the girl. "We're just catching up on all the hot gossip." She held up a celebrity magazine. "Actually, the magazine's a few months old. I guess it's cold gossip, at this point. Room temperature gossip."

There was a patient in the bed, sunken and still, with her eyes closed.

"Sorry, should we—" Hazel lowered her voice. "Shouldn't we be whispering?"

"Quite the opposite," said the girl. "The whole reason I'm here is so that Mary doesn't have to be alone. Voices are supposed to be good for them. Coma patients, I mean." She smiled warmly. "I'm Nisha, by the way. Student volunteer, not doting daughter. Despite the clear family resemblance."

That was a joke, Hazel was pretty sure, though her exhaustion was making it hard to tell. Pale skinned and small framed, Mary didn't bear any resemblance to Nisha. Hazel's eyes drifted over to the sac of fluid hanging above the bed, connected to Mary's arm with a tube.

"I'm Hazel. It's kind of you, visiting with her."

Nisha's smile grew playful. "Well, Hazel, as much as I'd like to accept the praise, I feel compelled to be honest with you. Volunteering is mandatory at my school, and yes, I know that 'mandatory volunteering' is an oxymoron. I'm guessing you don't go to Sacred Silence?"

"Uh, no." Hazel shook her head. "Gideon." She felt a little thrown off-balance by Nisha's effortless good humor. *Here* was a person who passed all her charisma checks.

"Well, at Sacred Silence, seventh and eighth graders have to complete fifty hours of community service, and since I procrastinated during sign-ups, I got last choice. Literally last choice in my entire grade. Don't tell Mary," she said, stage-whispering now, "but it turns out spending time with coma patients is a less popular pastime than picking up trash on the side of the highway."

Hazel smirked. "They should put that on the sign out front."

That got a laugh from Nisha—a full-throated cackle—and Hazel blushed, uncertain that she had really earned it. It had been Nisha's joke, really, and Hazel's quiet sarcasm rarely elicited much of a response.

That was partially by design. Hazel didn't love prolonged attention. She continued to blush under Nisha's regard. Her cheeks buzzed and her eye tingled.

Wait—how long had her eye been tingling?

Now that she noticed it, Hazel realized her sixth sense had been going for a while now. It was faint, but the background buzz was getting steadily more pronounced.

"I . . . s-sorry," Hazel said, and she covered her eye. "I get . . . migraines." She shoved her mom's brown-bag lunch toward the girl. "Can you get this to my mom? Her name's Nurse Grey. No, I mean, Nurse Sheridan."

Nisha looked skeptical, but she took the bag from Hazel. "You don't have your mom's name, you know, memorized?"

"Divorce!" Hazel said, so brightly that it felt weird. She gave a little half-shrug as she left the room. The tingling was nearly all-consuming at this point, demanding her full attention, but she had just enough self-awareness left to feel embarrassed about the extremely awkward exit.

She tried desperately to isolate a sense of direction in the buzzing. Could their supernatural sense actually guide them to relics, like some sort of psychic compass? That would be tremendously useful.

But the sensation was shapeless, radiating out from her orbital socket in waves. Facing different directions didn't affect the feeling at all.

Perhaps Hazel shouldn't even *try* to follow it, at least not while she was alone. She remembered the burst of pain she'd experienced when she took Detective Pryce's card. The spooky sense was unpredictable at the best of times, and now they knew

it could even be used against them. And if she was being honest, Hazel's sense was the least reliable of all.

She nearly turned around right there. She was so tired, and clearly in over her head. She could come back tomorrow, after a good night's sleep. Investigate the hospital in earnest.

But then Hazel saw Clara.

It was a fleeting glimpse: blond hair and an impish smile. A conspiratorial look that Hazel remembered well. It seemed to say, *Sure, we can watch something scary. But you can't tell your mom.*

And then the teen was gone, disappeared around a far corner.

If it weren't for the buzzing behind her eye, Hazel might have assumed she was mistaken. Perhaps a patient or another volunteer simply looked like Clara.

But Hazel knew that this was a vision. Emrys and Serena had both already experienced moments like these. Ghosts or echoes or whatever. In fact, Emrys's encounter with the specter of Brian Skupp had been what prompted them to seek out and stop his killer.

Hazel had been slower to acclimate to the Order's second sight than her friends. Whatever otherworldly sensitivity they possessed in spades, she had apparently lacked it. If this was what the experience was like, perhaps she should count herself lucky.

Still, she had to follow—had to see what Clara wanted to show her.

Hazel walked down the hallway in a sort of daze, trusting the vision to give her a clue and willing herself not to slip out of the dream state until she'd seen it. At some point, she entered a concrete stairwell; there she saw Clara again, descending the staircase. She briefly looked back at Hazel, but this time her mischievous expression had turned uneasy. The girl's form looked less solid now, less real. Was the vision already fading? The more Hazel tried to hold on to it, the faster it seemed to evaporate.

Clara glided down the stairs and was gone.

Hazel hurried after her and soon she found herself in the hospital basement, pushing through a set of heavy doors. The room beyond was empty but not silent. From nearby came a faint sound of knocking.

"H-hello?" asked Hazel. "Clara?" But she knew better than to expect an answer.

The harsh fluorescent lighting faltered, as if shuddering with cold. Hazel held her breath; there were no windows. If those lights failed, she would be plunged into total darkness.

Again, the sound of knocking. It was rhythmic, two knocks followed by a pause, and then again. It was a beat Hazel recognized but couldn't put a name to. And it was coming from a metal cabinet set against the far wall.

Hazel crept forward. The lights flickered, threatening to cut out completely. She reached for the cabinet's handle, and her hand trembled.

She realized what the sound was in the instant before she pulled open the door. Too late to stop herself.

It was a *heartbeat*.

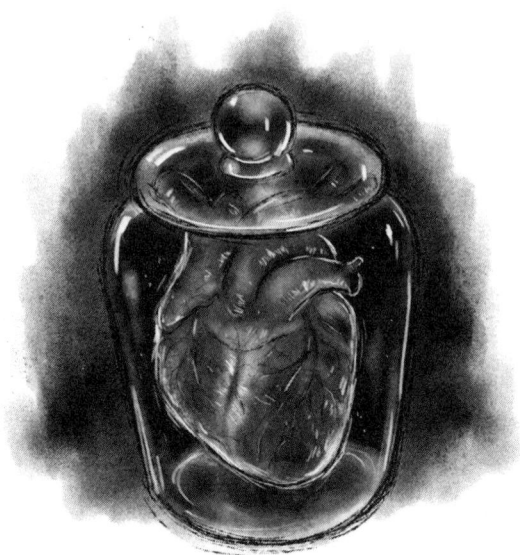

There within the cabinet, set amongst dozens of gruesome specimens, was a human heart, gory with blood and beating as fiercely as Hazel's own.

She stumbled backward, barely suppressing a scream.

And then a strong, heavy hand clamped down on her shoulder.

Five-Pointed Fright

🔒

From the New Rotterdam Wiki Project

There have long been rumors that New Rotterdam's **Five Points** district harbors a secret portal to hell, one that occasionally swallows any unfortunate bystander who stumbles upon it. Though the exact origin of the legend remains murky, most tellings connect it to the deadly **New Rotterdam Witch Trials**, when **Sarah Blackthorne** and nine others were executed on spurious evidence of witchcraft. Indeed, the Five Points district was the site of Sarah's execution. A plaque commissioned by the **New Rotterdam Cultural Institute** now memorializes its location.

Some have claimed that the portal opened to draw Sarah's wayward soul to its infernal torment. However, recent biographical evidence suggesting that **Gideon de Ruiter** may have fabricated the charges as a way of solidifying his political power have resulted in a popular counter-theory—that the gate is a punishment for the innocents killed by the young community.

Whatever the case, the bustling commercial and residential district remains an area of intense local speculation. Stories of the portal's exact location vary, as does its form, but all feature a mysterious hallway that appears as if from nowhere, from which strange light can be seen flickering around a distant corner. Frequently the hall smells of brimstone, and in many versions, its walls are marked with bizarre sigils, though whether the symbols are carved, drawn, or even spray-painted varies from source to source.

Frequently, a piteous voice can be heard from around the corner, beckoning for help. But in every telling, anyone who passes down the hallway is never seen again.

In popular culture

Author J. B. Goodheart popularized the legend in his story "What Waits Around the Corner," in which the story's narrator is drawn through a winding corridor by several increasingly desperate cries. As the unnamed narrator advances, however, his account becomes progressively more disturbed, ending in his realization that the voice crying out was his own.

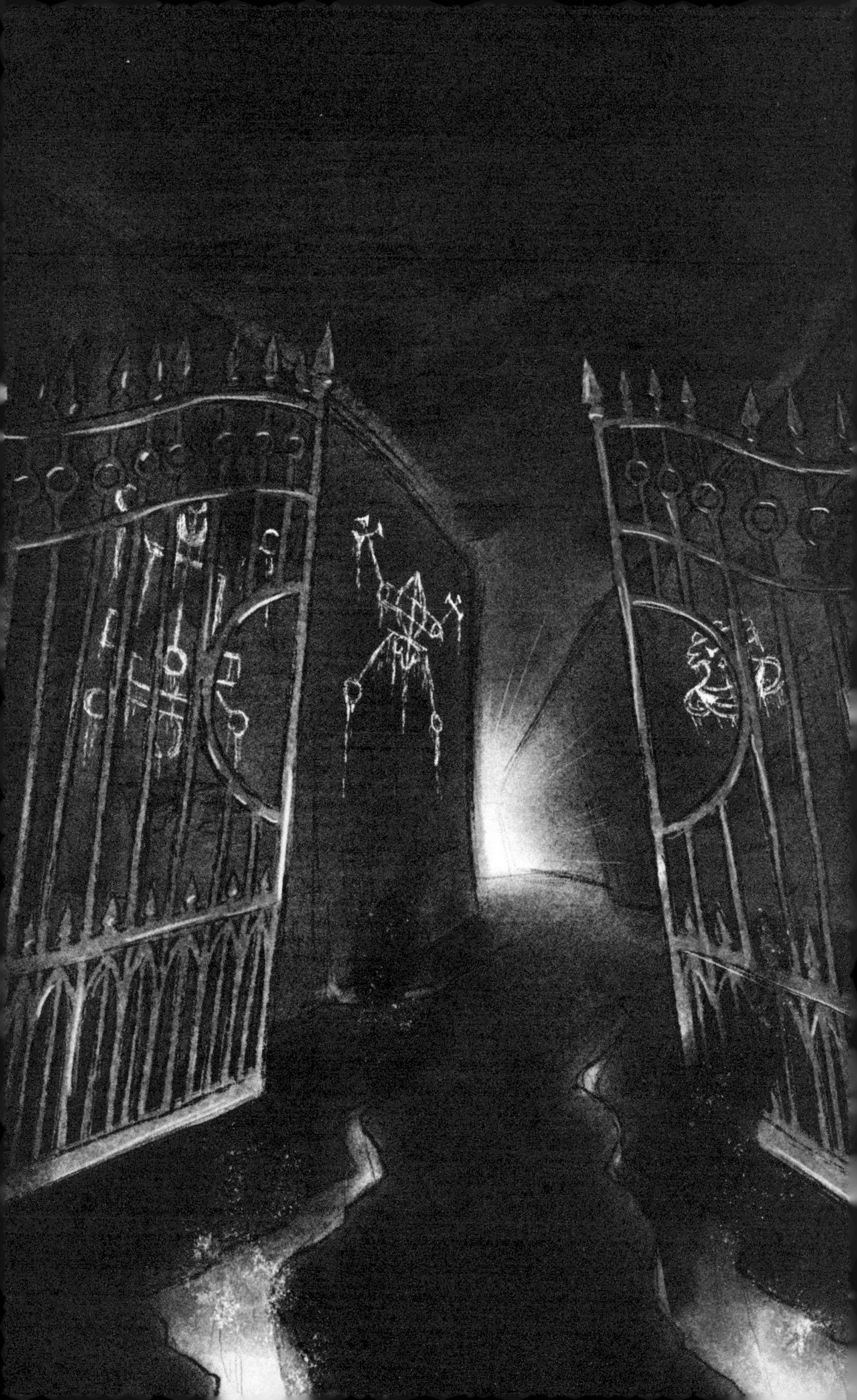

7

Hazel had never been a particularly acrobatic child. Like any sensible person, she preferred to keep her feet firmly on the ground. So it came as something of a surprise that she'd managed to leap as high as she did, shrieking the whole way up.

The hand gripping her shoulder released immediately, and soon Hazel found herself standing face-to-face with a very contrite-looking older gentleman.

"I am *so* sorry," the man said, holding his hands up in a gesture of apology. "I tried calling out to you, but you didn't appear to hear me. It seemed like . . . like you were in distress."

Distress was one word for it. Hazel's heart felt like it might pound right out of her—

She snapped around to where the dismembered heart had been beating an eerie rhythm just moments ago. But now the metal cabinet was empty of *any* body parts. The heart was gone, as were the unsettling jars full of other mysterious organs—innards turned out-ards. In their place were shelves brimming with gauze, bandages, and hypoallergenic gloves.

The vision was gone.

Hazel turned back to the man, slowly shaking her head.

"No," she said. "*I'm* sorry. I thought . . . I thought I heard something strange down here, but it must have been my imagination."

"Are you a patient at the hospital?" the man asked gently.

Hazel shook her head again. "My mom's a nurse here," she said. "She was so tired this morning that she forgot her lunch. I just came to drop it off." A lunch she'd practically thrown at that poor volunteer, Nisha, when her vision began. Hazel wondered if she should go and sheepishly retrieve it.

"A nurse!" the man said. "How wonderful. She works in the old wing, then? The one above us? I've had my eye on renovating it for some time."

"Renovating . . . ?" Hazel's eyes widened and her mouth fell open. "You're Julius Worthmann."

The man's kindly smile brightened. "You've heard of me? Ah, right. My name is on the new pediatric wing. Not *my* idea, mind you. The board insisted."

Hazel couldn't believe she was speaking to an actual billionaire. She'd assumed money like that made a person untouchable, like a shield that held the rest of the world at bay. Weren't billionaires too important to wander hospital basements without an entourage of armed guards? She glanced around but didn't see anyone else present.

"Not to be rude," Hazel said, "but what are you doing down *here*? Aren't you rich and famous? There are much nicer parts of the hospital to visit."

Worthmann chuckled. "I suppose I am rich. But famous? I'd hope not! Oh, I know a handful of magnates have enjoyed converting money into celebrity, but that's a particular brand of alchemy I'm entirely uninterested in." He winked.

At the word *alchemy*, Hazel grimaced inwardly. Her fingers twitched toward her pocket, where the Magnus Crown was hidden in its disguised state. She was suddenly aware that she was alone with this man in a creepy old basement. For all she knew, Worthmann could be a member of the Yellow Court.

He could even be the person responsible for killing Clara.

It wouldn't be the first time an apparently kind grown-up had turned a relic against innocent people. Hazel searched her senses for the strange pressure that indicated something supernatural was nearby, but her spooky sense had disappeared along with the vision of the heart.

Still, that vision had meant something. This place was connected to Clara's death; Hazel was sure of it. Perhaps a relic—or whoever was using it—lurked nearby. Whether she could sense them or not.

"Fame so easily becomes infamy," Julius Worthmann continued. "And I've found that a certain amount of anonymity enables a more . . . comfortable life. Like right now! None of the hospital staff have recognized me yet, allowing me to examine the building's foundations freely."

He glanced up, gazing appreciatively at the centuries-old stonework. "It's quite the place, isn't it? Yes, there are more modern facilities in the hospital complex, but there's so much history here. History that I'd see restored. This wing is the heart of the hospital."

Again, Hazel forced herself not to flinch. It was like Worthmann was reading her mind. Was that possible? Nothing seemed entirely outlandish anymore.

"What's your interest in the hospital?" she asked, attempting to keep her tone conversational. "Are you a history buff?"

Worthmann nodded absently, his eyes still scanning the room. "I suppose I am. This town has so many interesting stories, though many are sad ones. For instance, did you know that in its very first year, the hospital's head doctor was brutally murdered?"

A shiver ran down Hazel's spine. Of course he was. This was New Rotterdam.

"But perhaps it's too upsetting a story for someone so young," Worthmann said uncertainly, his eyes finally finding Hazel's.

Hazel shook her head. "My friends and I are big horror fans," she said. "It takes a lot to scare me."

Worthmann peered at her, as if discerning her courage with a look. Finally, he cleared his throat. "A birth had gone badly," he said. "The wife and unborn child of an important man both died. Three days later, the mummers arrived."

At Hazel's look of confusion, the man chuckled. "I'm not surprised you haven't heard of them. Mummers are an old tradition, brought over with the flood of British settlers in the 1800s. Traveling bands of actors—their faces obscured by masks or hoods—they roamed from house to house, enacting scenes. Usually, they depicted a mock death, wherein the deceased is magically resurrected. A bit of wish fulfillment, I suppose. But the mummers' plays also had a grimmer aspect. With their faces hidden, some used anonymity to commit terrible acts."

"Like murder?" Hazel asked.

Worthmann nodded. "A band of men arrived at the hospital one night, dressed in costumes, their faces covered. They coaxed the doctor outside and enacted a gruesome scene. They seized the man . . . and executed him in full view of the crowd that had gathered."

Worthmann paused, a hesitant look crossing his face. He must have worried he'd upset her.

"What happened to them?" she prompted. She needed to know more. Could this story be connected to Clara's death somehow?

"They fled into the darkness," Worthmann said. "Not one was ever brought to justice."

"That's horrible," Hazel rasped.

"Yes, it was an inauspicious start for the hospital," Worthmann said. "But a fascinating story, nonetheless."

Hazel shuddered, thinking of the poor doctor. She'd need to research the story more. Perhaps his ghost was still haunting the area surrounding the hospital, seeking revenge against his killers.

"I should get back," she said, inching toward the stairwell. "But it was nice to meet you, Mr. Worthmann."

"You, too, Miss . . . ?"

"Hazel," she said. "Hazel Grey."

"Miss Grey. And your mother . . . you said she was a nurse here. What's *her* name?"

Hazel froze. For a moment, she wondered if she'd inadvertently gotten her mom in trouble, poking around where she wasn't supposed to. Worthmann was important here, after all.

But the man smiled warmly. "Perhaps I can put in a good word. I know a few of the bosses, after all." He winked again.

"Lisa Sheridan," Hazel said hesitantly. "But, sir, if that's true . . . what my mom could really use is more staff. She's been running twelve-hours shifts for nearly two weeks now, because there's no one else to cover when something goes wrong. The ER needs money. It needs you."

Worthmann nodded, a contemplative look touching his eyes. Then he tapped his temple. "I'll try to remember that. Goodbye, Miss Grey. And thank you for sharing your perspective."

Hazel backed out of the room, her mind whirring. She hoped she hadn't just complicated her mom's life further. But despite all the griping she'd heard about Julius Worthmann, the man had seemed thoughtful and attentive—even kind. Perhaps all he needed was to hear from someone on the ground.

Still, right this moment, what *Hazel* needed was to get home. Both the vision and her encounter with Worthmann had left her absolutely sapped. Hopefully Emrys and Serena had found a VCR by now. At the very least, she had quite a story to tell *them*.

Winter of 1636 🔒

From the New Rotterdam Wiki Project

> *"Winter's Winnowing"* redirects here.

On November 13, 1636, three months after departing the Netherlands and thousands of miles from its intended destination of Florida, the Dutch galleon Volle Maan dropped anchor off the coast of modern-day New Rotterdam.

The ship's travel-weary passengers were ill-prepared for the region, a fact that became apparent as winter descended. The first snows came early, before food and firewood stockpiles could be established. Local wildlife harassed the settlers, evading their hunting parties by day and stalking the settlement by night. On one occasion, a coyote plucked an unattended baby from its crib. The child's mother, responding too late to the babe's cries, swore the animal had stood upright as it loped back into the fog-enshrouded forest.

Starvation and exposure further winnowed the settlers' numbers, and the winter showed no signs of abating.

Gideon de Ruiter, de facto leader of the settlement due to his role in the October Mutiny, barricaded himself away for untold days to pray for a solution. In his absence, a young settler, Virginia Vellekoop, stepped into a leadership role. Her pragmatic problem-solving had an immediately positive effect on morale.

When de Ruiter emerged from isolation, however, he made a startling claim. Virginia, he insisted, was a witch, in league with the foul primordial spirits of this harsh and unwelcoming land. According to de Ruiter, she had orchestrated the settlement's misfortunes in order to advance her own standing. Based on de Ruiter's word alone, Virginia was exiled.

Still, there were some among the settlers who believed in Virginia's innocence. Though they would not stand up to de Ruiter, they did what they could to help her, leaving blankets beneath trees and precious bits of bread upon their windowsills.

Months passed, and with the first thaw of spring, the settlement counted their dead. All told, four dozen souls had been lost to the winter.

Everyone agreed that Virginia Vellekoop was among them. Yet no body was ever found. And for years to come, children of the village would swear they saw a young woman matching Virginia's description peering at them through closed shutters, particularly on cold nights when the fires of New Rotterdam's hearths glowed bright.

8

Hazel hadn't intended to try to use the Crown again so soon. But by the time she got home, Emrys and Serena were busy—dinner with their families—and, exhausted as she was, sleep seemed impossible. Every time she so much as blinked, she saw that disembodied heart again, or else Clara's ghostly face. What would she see if she fully closed her eyes? How could her dreams show her anything but horror now?

Instead, she turned on every light in the apartment. She couldn't control where her dreams would take her, or whatever *visions* her new senses had in store for her, but she could keep her mind from wandering by focusing on a task. The thornier the task, the better. Which made the Magnus Crown the natural choice.

She found some old costume jewelry she'd been gifted years ago by a distant aunt. The bracelet was pure tin, she was fairly certain—and tin was just one row above lead on the periodic table. If her theory held, then transmuting one metal to another should just be a matter of concentration and time—plus whatever metabolic energy the Crown required from her. She drank a soda to get her blood sugar up, and she looked at atomic models for the two metals online, to help her wrap her head around the science of what she was about to do.

The minutes passed, torturously slow, as Hazel focused all her concentration on the tin bracelet. She worried she'd burst a blood vessel in her eye if she stared any harder. On two occasions, she sensed, more than saw, a scarlet glow at the edge of her perception. But when she glanced to her periphery, it was gone.

She could almost feel the relic resisting her efforts, pushing back as it had before. Or was that her imagination? Maybe it was easier to imagine the relic was adversarial than to accept she just wasn't getting it.

She was so absorbed in her task that she almost missed the sound of knocking at her front door. Tossing a hand towel over the jewelry, she ran out of her room, crossed the apartment, and peered through the peephole.

It was Serena and Emrys. Had she missed a text? A glance at her phone revealed she'd missed several, in fact.

Hazel cast a quick look around. The den was a mess, with dirty clothes piled on the sofa and takeout containers from who-knew-when cluttering up the side tables. She knew the kitchen was no better; she still hadn't gotten around to those dishes.

"One second!" she cried, and for a mad moment she actually considered opening a portal to the Archive and shoving all the mess across the dimensional divide.

In the end, she settled on spraying some air freshener. It was the best she could do in the time it took Serena to start kicking impatiently at the door.

Hazel unlatched the door, and Serena burst into the entryway clutching a massive rectangular bulk of machinery. "Success!" she announced.

"Is that a VCR?" Hazel said. "We're doing this *here*? What's wrong with your apartment?"

"Dom's home," Serena said matter-of-factly, steering the equipment around Hazel and toward the den. "You can probably smell the flatulence from here."

All Hazel could smell was the "fresh linen" scent she'd saturated the air with. She'd definitely overdone it.

"Hi, sorry," Emrys said from the threshold. He was holding a plate wrapped in tinfoil. "We figured we should have privacy for this, and since your mom's still at work . . ."

"Invite the poor boy inside!" said Serena. She was already poking around behind Hazel's TV for the necessary connections. "The way he lurks in doorways, I think he might be a vampire. I'm putting it on the wiki!"

Hazel sighed. Even in the face of all they'd seen, Serena still enjoyed poking fun at the wiki. As if Hazel and Emrys just posted random flights of fancy.

"He's not a vampire; he's just got actual manners. It's okay, Emrys," said Hazel. "Come in. What's that?"

Emrys held out the plate. "Leftover quiche. My dad insisted

I bring some over when I told him your mom was working all day. I told him you probably ate already . . ."

At the mention of food, her traitorous stomach growled loudly. "I lost track of time, actually. I've been experimenting with my relic." She took the plate from Emrys. "Thanks."

From Serena, the food might have felt like charity. From Mr. Houtmann, good-natured and guileless, she could accept it as a simple gesture of kindness.

Emrys bounced on his toes. "Experimenting with your relic? Any luck?"

Hazel huffed. "No, actually. Which is even more frustrating now, because as far as I can tell, I'm doing the same exact thing that worked last time." She took a bite of quiche; it was still warm. "Getting repeatable results is the whole foundation of the scientific method," she added, covering her mouth to avoid spitting crumbs at Emrys.

Van Stavern's voice sounded from within Emrys's tote. "It certainly sounds as if there are interesting developments in the world above. Alas, it appears forever my lot to dwell alone in darkness."

"Oop, sorry!" said Emrys, and he scrambled to remove the book.

Serena tutted from behind Hazel's TV. "What's the Dewey decimal number for melodrama, Alyx?" she asked. "We need to make sure we shelve you appropriately."

The book huffed with indignation, but composed itself as it

turned its single eye onto Hazel. "Perhaps I heard incorrectly," he said. "Don't tell me you remain determined to impose a limiting rational worldview upon one of the great and boundless thaumaturgic wonders of the Middle Ages?"

"I don't see why not." Hazel shrugged. "The philosopher's stone transmutes the elements, supposedly, and elements are known scientific quantities. Elements are made of atoms, and atoms are made of protons, neutrons, and electrons. If I know that lead has an atomic number of 82, and gold has an atomic number of 79, then it should be just a matter of removing three protons, and—"

"I see your error," said Van Stavern, and Hazel bristled at his choice of words. "Alchemy may have the *trappings* of a science, but it is best understood as an art. They call it the philosopher's stone and not the physicist's stone, after all. The alchemists of yore saw their pursuit as a *spiritual* endeavor."

"Spiritual?" asked Emrys. "Like, religious? What's that got to do with transmutation?"

"The alchemists sought to turn a common, undesirable metal—lead—into something beautiful and valuable and pure," answered Van Stavern. "Likewise, they hoped to purify their souls, to rise above the petty baseness and sinfulness of humanity and prove themselves worthy of Heaven. They thought that achieving one would accomplish the other; elevate *matter* and you elevate the *soul*."

"I get it," said Emrys. "It's like a metaphor. When they're

talking about 'base metals,' they were really talking about their supposedly sinful souls."

"Just so," said Van Stavern. "A little more poetry, a little less *atomic arithmetic*. Emrys has the right idea."

Hazel just barely managed to avoid saying something snarky. Van Stavern had definitely selected his star student; Hazel wanted to be happy for Emrys, but she only felt annoyed. Left behind.

"I don't know, 'atomic arithmetic' sounds pretty cool to me," said Serena. She had stepped away from the electronics to fully join the conversation. "Let's not all dogpile on Hazel, okay? She'll get it in her own time."

Hazel bristled at that, too. Serena made her sound like she was a remedial math student. Like she needed to be held back after class for tutoring.

Not that there was anything wrong with that, but Hazel was used to being the tutor, not the struggling student.

"We're not ganging up on you," Emrys said, concern in his eyes. "Right? I just want to help."

"We all do," Van Stavern agreed. "Every member of the Order develops their own sort of relationship with the unseen world, and at their own pace. Emrys's spell-casting methodology is far less disciplined—" He faltered at Serena's dirty look. "That is to say, he is far more intuitive than any sorcerer I've ever met. Serena likewise has surprised me with her natural sensitivity to the subtle forces that move the supernatural world. A rare and encouraging gift."

Hazel blushed. Van Stavern seemed to have praise for everyone but her. Next he'd tell them that Emrys's dog had mastered a relic and had the Yellow Court in full retreat.

"Hey. Chatterbox." Serena fairly glared at the book. "I said that's enough." She turned her gaze on Hazel, her expression softening. "Hazel has updates for us. I want to hear about this awkward encounter at the hospital."

Hazel's blushing deepened. Had Serena heard about her conversation with that volunteer? How? "It . . . it wasn't *that* awkward."

Serena arched an eyebrow. "You were cornered by a shady billionaire in an off-limits area of the hospital and he told you a story about a murderous mime or something? It sounds a little uncomfortable to me."

"Oh, right," said Hazel. She'd momentarily forgotten she'd texted Emrys and Serena about meeting Worthmann.

"Not a mime," said Emrys. "A mummer." He held up his phone, showing a wiki page that documented the events of Worthmann's story. "And we're definitely on the right track. Listen to this . . . the mummers didn't just kill the doctor. They cut out his *heart*."

Hazel gasped. Worthmann hadn't mentioned *that* gruesome detail. The story must be connected to Clara!

"You said you had a vision?" Serena prompted.

Hazel shuddered at the memory. "It was unsettling. But *whatever's* happening, the hospital's at the center of it."

"The hospital," said Serena. "And Worthmann."

"No, I—" Hazel faltered. "It was a weird conversation, but it wasn't *sinister*. And why would he give us a clue? Why spend his money to make the hospital a better place?"

"For the tax write-off," said Serena. "Or the ego boost. Believe me, whatever he's spending on *good works*, it's a fraction of what he could do. There's no such thing as an altruistic billionaire. His gifts come with strings attached."

Hazel couldn't help but note the irony. Money complicated relationships. It was exactly why she'd avoided asking Serena for help with the convention ticket.

"Speaking of gifts," Emrys said, looking down at his phone. "Worthmann was a major contributor to Mayor Royce's campaign."

"That seals it," said Serena.

"No, it doesn't," said Hazel. "More than half of New Rotterdam voted for Royce."

"More than half of the *adults*," Serena countered.

"All the same, they can't all be in the Yellow Court."

Serena sniffed. "They're lousy judges of character, at the very least. But why are you so certain Worthmann's innocent?"

Because I need him to be, thought Hazel. *Because he can make my mom's job easier.*

But she said: "I'm not sure of anything."

"We need more to go on," said Emrys.

"Well, there is this," said Serena, and she waved the VHS tape at them. "Although it's not the movie night I was hoping for."

Hazel's heart sank as Serena popped the tape in. She didn't relish the idea of seeing Clara's final hours for herself. As a fuzzy overhead view of the Grinning Gas's interior appeared on her screen, she felt like she was spying on the girl behind the counter.

Not that there was much to see. Clara spent most of the shift on her phone. Even when Serena pressed the fast-forward button, the girl barely seemed to move; just her thumbs, trailing across the phone screen and tapping out texts. At one point, she began playing with a fidget spinner; from above, the toy made an almost hypnotic pattern, but even that didn't tear Clara's focus away from her phone.

And then, something changed. Clara suddenly jolted; her gaze was drawn toward the front of the store. She'd seen something beyond the glass storefront, and she seemed ready to run in the other direction.

Serena set the tape to its normal speed. The picture suddenly became clearer, though not by much. Hazel had grown used to the faster speed, so Clara's hesitation seemed to drag on for ages.

But Clara suddenly smiled, no longer fearful of whatever she'd seen. She stepped out from behind the counter and ran toward the front doors. She was so eager that she fumbled with the lock for several long seconds; then, she threw open the door and hurried outside.

They left the tape running for some time after that. But Clara never reappeared.

"That was the moment," Serena said. "It must have been. Whoever or whatever killed her was just outside the station."

"I don't understand," said Emrys. "She was safer inside. Why did she open the door? Why go outside at all?"

Hazel turned to her friends. "She didn't just go outside. She ran out with a smile on her face." Hazel's tongue felt thick and heavy. "The killer . . . it was someone she knew. Someone she trusted."

Serena scowled. "And if the police have the tape from the front parking lot, then they know exactly who's responsible. Awfully suspicious that they claim to have no leads."

"Forget the police," said Hazel. "They're in on it. This is up to us, and I've got an idea about what we do next." She stood and walked to the kitchen, and when her friends followed, she forgot to even be self-conscious about the state of the dishes. Witnessing the final moments of Clara's life had forced most other thoughts from her mind.

"How do you feel about community service?" Hazel asked.

"I love it," said Serena. "Particularly when other people do it."

"The hospital's at the center of whatever's happening," Hazel said, and she picked up two sheets of paper from the counter, handing one to each of her friends.

Emrys read aloud from the top of his sheet. "Volunteer application form?" He got it right away. "So we can get access to Saint Azazel. Brilliant!"

Hazel allowed herself to enjoy the compliment; it was her favorite one. "There's a pen clipped to the calendar."

Serena, who was closest to the wall calendar, grabbed the pen. Her eyes lingered on the color-coded squares.

"Mom's work schedule," Hazel explained. "It's enough to make your head spin."

"She's working every weekend for the rest of the month," Serena said.

"Yeah," said Hazel. "It's really—"

"She's working on RotterCon weekend," Serena said. She turned an accusing look on Hazel. "You said she was spending the weekend with you."

"I—" Hazel faltered. "Her schedule keeps changing, and—"

"Hazel, stop lying," Serena said.

Serena's command fell between them like a land mine. They all went completely still. Emrys looked like he was afraid to even breathe.

"What's going on with you?" Serena asked. "Is this because you're having a hard time with your relic? Because I'm sure with a little more time—"

"It isn't that," Hazel said. "I just . . . I don't want to go to RotterCon. We've got more important things to worry about."

"Like keeping a cult of nihilists from abusing inconceivably powerful relics, I know," said Serena. "But we can't work nonstop, or we'll end up like your mom."

Hazel gritted her teeth. "And what exactly is wrong with my mom?"

"Nothing," Serena said, hands raised in apology. "That's not what I meant. I only meant that self-care is—"

"Oh my god, Serena! If you say 'self-care' at me one more time, I'll scream!" She was sort of already screaming, she realized, but she couldn't stop now; Serena had stepped on the land mine; she should have expected an explosion. "I'm sure my mom would rather do hot yoga in a cucumber mask or *whatever* than work sixty hours a week, but she doesn't have a choice! Not that you could understand that."

"I understand plenty," said Serena. "And I can tell when I'm being iced out. I thought accepting a cursed relic and joining this doomed knitting circle would fix things between us, but you're still pushing me away."

"I'm not," Hazel said, instinctively pushing back against the accusation, but she didn't know how to finish the thought. *Had* she been pushing Serena away? Their friendship had changed when Emrys had moved into the building. But Emrys and Serena had worked through their issues. Defeating a child-eating monster together would do that.

Hazel assumed so, anyway. She hadn't been there for that part.

The anger that had fueled her evaporated all at once. Like an engine running on fumes, her side of the argument sputtered to a stop.

That's just what it was like, arguing with Serena. Maybe that's what Van Stavern had been getting at when he'd called her "truth-seeker." She had a way of cutting right to the heart of things.

"I'm tired," Hazel said. "I don't even know what I'm saying."

Seeing Hazel's exhausted face, Serena softened slightly.

Emrys cleared his throat, as if reminding them that he was there. "I, uh, think we're all tired. And stressed. It's been a really difficult day." He waved his volunteer form like a white flag. "And we should get our parents to sign this before they go to bed."

"Yeah," Serena agreed. She smiled a little half smile in Hazel's direction, a tentative apology. "It really is a brilliant plan."

"Thanks," Hazel said. But somehow, this time, the compliment rang hollow to her ears.

The Last Mummers' Play 🔒

From the New Rotterdam Wiki Project

Brought to New Rotterdam with the wave of British settlers, mummers' plays are folk plays performed by troupes of amateur actors, traditionally all male, known as mummers. Historically, mummers' plays consisted of informal groups of costumed community members that visited from house to house on various holidays.

However, in the autumn of 1872, one such play was conducted with murderous intent, following the deaths of Lizbeth de Ruiter and her stillborn child. Lizbeth was the daughter of British immigrants, and had recently married into the prestigious de Ruiter family, taking Kees de Ruiter as her husband, along with his name.

Rather than hiring a midwife and conducting the birth at home, as was common practice at the time, Kees and Lizbeth were persuaded to attend the newly founded Saint Azazel Hospital, under the care of its first head physician, Doctor Tielman 't Hart. Tragically, Lizbeth's was a breech birth, and both she and the child were lost. By all accounts, Kees was devastated, as was Lizbeth's sizable family.

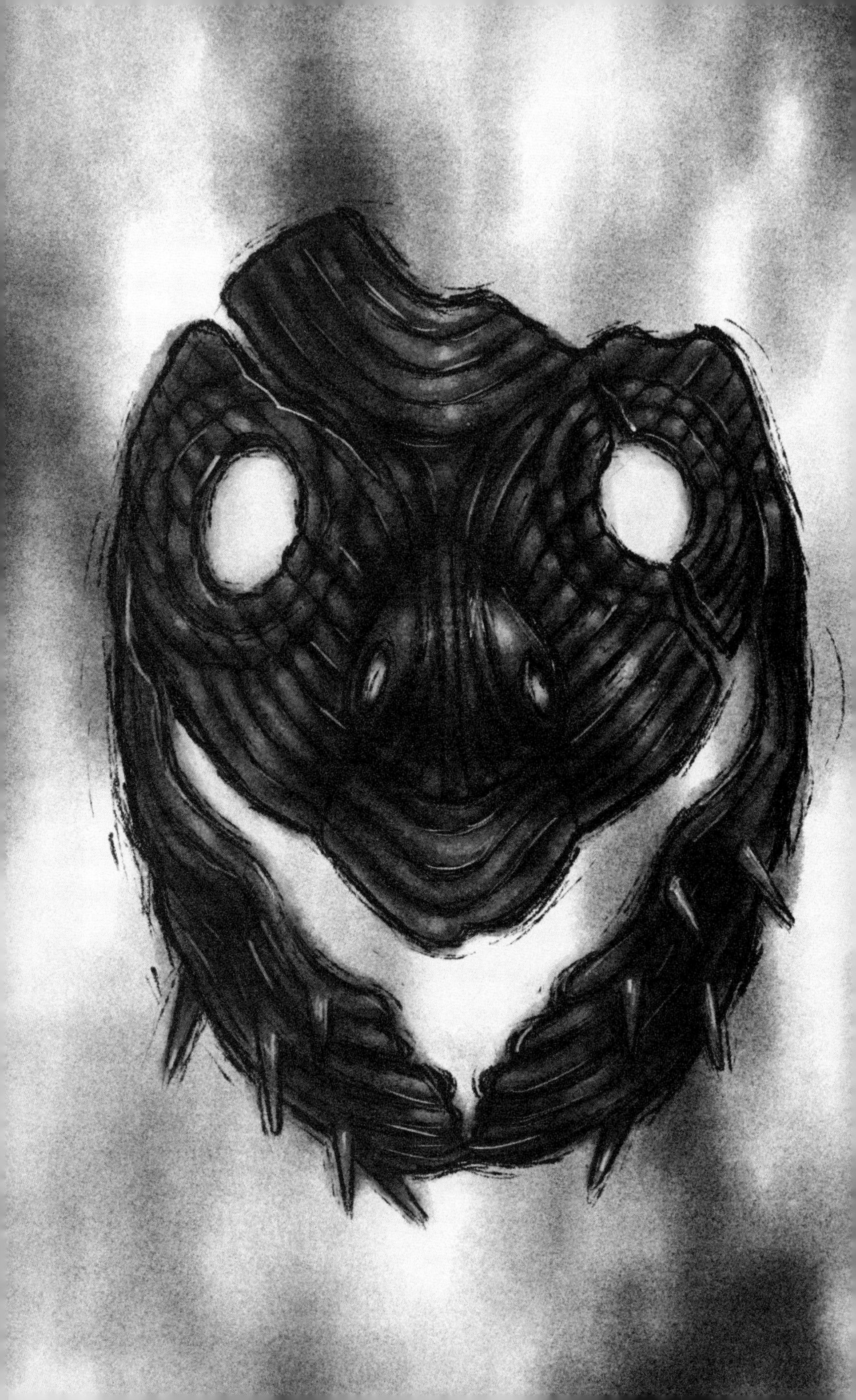

Three days later, on October 29, 1872, a troupe of mummers was seen traveling around the town, visiting houses and conducting their show. The mummers' play held to its usual format, a performance in which two characters engaged in a comic mock battle, where one was "slain" in the duel. A doctor character then emerged from the throng, revealing a magic potion that was used to resurrect the fallen duelist.

When the troupe reached the hospital, however, their performance abruptly changed. Doctor 't Hart was lured outside by the players, who quickly subdued the man and enacted a public cardiectomy, executing him in full view of witnesses by removing the doctor's heart. As the performance ended, the mummers revealed that there would be no miraculous resurrection, as the doctor himself was dead. They then fled into the nearby forest.

Legacy

No formal charges were ever brought against the murderers, and their identities were never confirmed. Many historians believe Kees de Ruiter was likely to blame, his family's prestige insulating him from prosecution. Others suspect Lizbeth's family may have been involved, though they denied any connection to the crime. While none of the masked mob were ever brought to justice, the New Rotterdam Secretary of the Commonwealth outlawed mummers' plays the very next year, effectively erasing the tradition from the region.

9

Despite her exhaustion, Hazel slept fitfully that night, her dreams a blur of masked murderers and bodiless hearts. She woke several times with the grisly images still imprinted on her eyelids, and had to wait out the fear that clung to her long after they'd faded.

Not for the first time, Hazel thought about how unfair this all was. Unfair that this task—fighting monsters and containing cursed relics—had fallen onto the shoulders of three kids. Emrys had never understood Serena's hesitance in accepting Van Stavern's charge, but Hazel did. Despite her fascination with the macabre, she knew what they were doing was deeply dangerous. And while Emrys was correct that ignoring the danger wouldn't make it go away, that didn't make it right that it was theirs alone to brave, either.

After her latest unpleasant awakening, a dream in which Clara's beating heart had appeared in Hazel's home, tucked amidst the dirty dishes in the sink, Hazel's throat felt raw. She reached for her bedside water glass but it was empty. Checking the clock, she saw it was nearly three in the morning. Tomorrow would be painful.

She slipped out of bed, carefully lifting the glass from the table, and crept from her room toward the kitchen.

Had Mom gotten home from work yet? Hazel hadn't heard her come in, but it was possible she'd slept through her arrival. She moved quietly, just in case. No need to inflict her sleeplessness on others.

In the kitchen, Hazel slowly edged on the faucet, careful to keep the stream as silent as possible.

She thought of Clara, and all the people who'd been harmed by the relics and the Yellow Court. People who'd been eaten alive by forces they couldn't begin to comprehend. At least Hazel and her friends *understood* the threats they were facing, and were armed against them. That understanding was worth a few nights of lost sleep. She resolved to stop feeling sorry for herself. So many people had it worse, in so many ways.

Hazel turned the faucet off just as the line of water climbed toward the glass's lip. She took a long swallow, her scratchy throat rejoicing. Then she turned and headed back toward her room.

"Hazel?"

Hazel snapped around.

Her mom's voice. She'd heard it coming from the stairs outside.

"Mom?" Hazel called unsurely.

There was a long tick of silence, then her mom's voice echoed up from the stairwell again, muffled through the thick apartment door.

"Hazel, can you come down, sweetie? I have something to show you."

"Mom, what are you doing out there?" Hazel set her water glass on the counter and switched on the living room lamp, moving toward the front door. She pulled it open, and the hall's motion-sensor light flickered on, bathing the stairway in cold fluorescent tones.

"I have a surprise for you, Hazel!" her mom's voice echoed up again. "It's right outside—come see!" Hazel heard the door to the building open and close, her mother retreating out front.

"What in the world?" Hazel whispered.

It was far too late for shouted conversations up the apartment stairway. She grabbed hold of the banister, but paused. Should she go back for her shoes? Hazel decided to continue barefoot for now. Her curiosity was officially piqued.

Down the stairs she went, past Serena's apartment on the third floor, finally arriving at the cramped first-floor vestibule. Bright light flooded in from the door's tiny window. It was a wonder none of the neighbors were complaining.

"Mom?" Hazel said.

"Out here, baby!" came her mom's voice from outside.

Hazel peered through the window and gasped.

There was her mom in a stylish outfit, one that Hazel was sure was brand-new.

"Hey, Hazel-bug!" Her mom grinned. "You'll never guess what happened."

Hazel dimly realized her mouth was hanging open. She managed to close it only with a great deal of effort.

Behind her mother, the car was idling, its headlights bright and cheery against the night's almost impenetrable darkness. But Hazel could see the back seat was chock-*full* of shopping bags. She couldn't read the logos from where she was, but recognized the shapes well enough to know that they represented expensive designer brands.

Hazel pushed the door open. "Mom, what are you *doing?*" she called down the stoop.

"It's happened, Hazel. I don't know what came over me, but I decided to buy a lotto ticket while getting gas on the way to work." Her mom shook her head, looking just as astonished as Hazel felt. "And I won! I used your birthday for the numbers. Can you believe it?"

Hazel *couldn't* believe it. She knew that the chances of winning the lottery were small enough as to make it nearly futile. The people who most needed the money bled themselves dry for what amounted to a statistical impossibility.

. . . But somebody had to win, right? And why *not* Hazel's mom? She worked so hard for their family. They both did.

"Things are about to change." Hazel's mom laughed. "Big-time. I'm going to quit nursing. Breathe a little. Finally, I'll be able to take care of *you*, rather than the other way around."

Hazel's eye stung. Before she knew it, tears were streaming down her cheeks.

"Aw, don't cry, honey!" her mom said. "Everything is finally getting better. And you can go to that scary movie convention with your friends!" She raised her arms, inviting Hazel in for a hug.

Hazel couldn't move fast enough. She took a hurried step forward, throwing the door wide open—

"Hazel?"

—when her mom's voice called from the hallway behind her, tight with worry and confusion.

Hazel turned slowly. There was her mother hovering on the staircase, looking exhausted and disheveled in her pajamas.

"Hazel, what are you *doing* out here?"

The fear that shot up Hazel's spine was unlike anything she'd ever experienced. The headlights beaming behind her melted suddenly into darkness, throwing the vestibule into pitch-black. Hazel spun around, but her mother, the car, the fancy shopping bags—*all* of them were gone.

And her right eye was buzzing furiously.

She cast about for some sign of them, but it was too dark to see anything.

No—there. A strange light bobbed in the distance, retreating

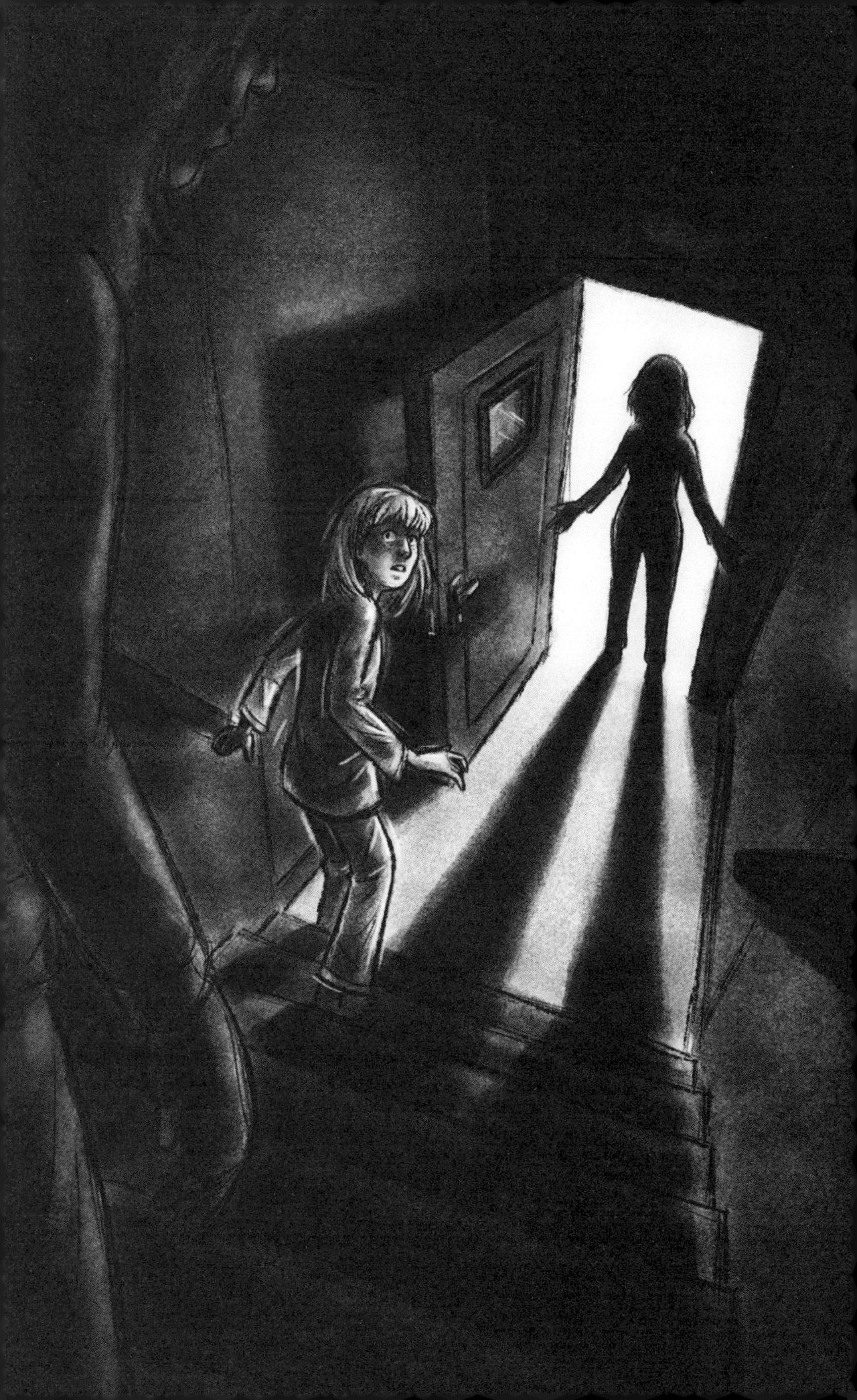

quickly into the shadows. Hazel squinted to get a better look, but it was gone in a moment.

Suddenly, her whole body began to shake. As her legs failed her, Hazel slowly sank to the ground.

"Sweetie!" Her mom rushed to her, wrapping Hazel in her arms. "What happened? Were you sleepwalking? I saw the light on and followed you out."

This was the thing that had hunted Clara—Hazel was sure. And just like in the surveillance video, it had nearly lured *her* to a similar fate. Just a moment or two more, and Hazel . . .

She'd be . . .

The disembodied heart from her nightmares flashed before her eyes.

Hazel let herself be enveloped in her mother's embrace, her body shivering uncontrollably.

"Sweetie!" her mom said again. "Hazel, what *happened*?"

What indeed?

So much for understanding the enemy.

✕

"And your mom didn't see any of it?" Emrys asked. "Not even the headlights?"

Hazel shook her head. It was the next morning, and she and her friends had gathered in the Blue Reliquary to debrief.

Once Hazel had finally stopped shaking the previous night, her mother had led her back upstairs to the apartment and made a piping-hot mug of tea. Hazel had run with the sleepwalking story, telling her mom that a particularly vivid dream must have drawn her from bed. When she'd asked if Hazel wanted to talk about it, though, Hazel had simply shaken her head and said she didn't remember.

Minutes later, while her mom puttered around the kitchen, Hazel had texted Emrys and Serena.

DA tomorrow morning. 7 sharp.

Then, to underscore the urgency, she added: *Just met Clara's killer.*

Both had arrived promptly at 6:59.

Serena now took Hazel's hand in hers, frowning worriedly. Her warmth and steadiness were a comfort. Hazel hadn't slept at all after the encounter. Her exhaustion from the day before was only compounded.

"Mom didn't see or hear anything," she said. "As far as I can tell, it was all in my mind." She took a deep, shuddering breath. "But it was so *real*. I could hear the way Mom's voice echoed off the tiles in the hallway. Everything, every detail, was perfect."

"Many powers can access our memories and alter our perceptions," Van Stavern said. The grimoire's intense blue stare hadn't shifted from Hazel during the entire conversation. "Wendigos, fairies—there are countless tales warning against following the voice that calls your name from beyond the fire's light. These relics make for particularly dangerous retrievals. You must guard yourselves against them as much as possible. Trust not even your own thoughts."

"How exactly are we supposed to fight something like that?" Serena asked.

"There are techniques to steel the mind among the Atlas's pages," Van Stavern said. "Meditations and mantras—though most require an ascetic lifestyle away from society and years of punishing physical trials. How do you feel about gruel?"

"Sorry I asked," Serena muttered, slouching in her seat.

Now the Atlas's eye finally broke from Hazel, turning to Serena.

"As it happens, however," Van Stavern said, "*your* relic is uniquely qualified for this undertaking."

Serena's eyebrows rose.

"If the relic's user is indeed hunting through hallucinatory means, the Aegis of Truth is our best tool for cutting through its deceptions. To put it simply, the relic can see through illusions."

"Just a reminder to everyone," Serena said, "but I've barely used the Aegis." She held the bangle up for all to see. In its hidden form, it resembled nothing more than a shiny accessory. Vintage, but hardly ancient. "There are no guarantees I'll be able to make it work."

"Thankfully," Van Stavern said, "unlike Emrys's Atlas or Hazel's Crown, many of the Aegis's primary powers are . . . let's say *baked into* the relic. You will still need practice to access its higher arts, however."

"So what?" Serena asked. "I just point the shield and go?"

"If by *go*, you mean peer through the relic's clarifying surface to reveal hidden truths, then . . . well, yes."

Hazel nodded slowly. "Sounds like you're our secret weapon," she said to Serena. Hazel pulled her hand from beneath her friend's palm, setting it onto her lap.

Serena frowned. "Are you all right?" she asked seriously. "Listen, if you want to talk about yesterday . . ."

Hazel shook her head. She was so tired. Perhaps even more so than yesterday. But she still understood that she'd been responsible for the fight. The truth was, Hazel *had* been keeping things from her friends, even going so far as to lie to them. It wasn't Serena's fault that she'd caught on.

How could they be expected to trust her in life-or-death situations, if Hazel wouldn't trust *them* with her mundane problems?

"I'm sorry," she said. "I'm sorry for pushing you away, and for getting jealous about your powers . . . and for lying about the convention."

Serena laughed. "I'm still not entirely sure what powers everyone is talking about, so let's put that apology on ice." She sat up straight, though her gaze fell to the table. "Hazel, I don't know what's going on with you—but maybe that's okay. You like to handle things on your own. I can respect that. But if it ever gets to be too much, you know Emrys and I have your back, right?"

Emrys nodded eagerly. "We love you, Hazel!"

The way he said the words seemed as easy as breathing. Hazel couldn't remember the last time she'd said them to anyone but her mother. Kids their age didn't say "I love you."

But hearing it filled her with a flood of emotions that she had a hard time navigating—guilt and gratitude crashed together with other feelings she couldn't put names to. Perhaps she didn't need to. Perhaps she could simply get lost in the flow.

"We love you," Serena repeated, her eyes having risen to meet Hazel's. "And we're here to support you, whenever and however we can."

Hazel nodded, her throat closing around whatever reply she might have made. If she wasn't so drained of tears from last night, she'd certainly be crying.

But they still had a murder to solve. Whatever she might be feeling, Hazel had to push her emotions down once again. For Clara's sake.

Last night, whatever had killed Clara had come after Hazel. It had offered her everything she wanted and more. Stability, support, financial security. These had been the lures used to draw her away from the safety of the fire. And in a small, dark place—deep at Hazel's core—she still felt the sting of their loss.

But Hazel wouldn't be fooled again. She knew the killer's tricks now.

"Thanks," she finally said. "That means a lot . . . truly. But right now, the best way you can support me is by stopping that *thing.*"

"We still don't know who they are," Emrys said.

"*I* still think Worthmann is the most likely candidate," Serena said, casting an apologetic glance at Hazel.

Hazel sighed and set her jaw. She was more exhausted than she'd ever been in her life, but every moment they let the killer roam free meant another potential victim like Clara.

"You're both right," she said. "We can't say for sure that it's Worthmann, but the fact that the killer came for me right after I met him is about as big a red flag as you can get. Still—we do know three things. The first is that Clara's death is connected to the hospital. Second, whoever or whatever killed her, they're luring their victims with the things they want most. So I say we take the hunt to the hunter. We set a lure of our own, right in their backyard."

Understanding dawned on Serena's face, but then it was quickly occluded by horror. "Hazel, *no*," she said.

Emrys glanced between them, looking confused. "What? What's wrong?"

Hazel sighed. "The last thing we know is what the killer wants: me. If we're going to trap them, we're going to need bait." Hazel set her hands on the table. "And I'm the best lure we've got."

Nana Faye's Family Recipe

From the New Rotterdam Wiki Project

For decades, the New Rotterdam County Fair and Agricultural Exhibition was famously consistent. Attendees could count on riding the same rickety rides, forever seeming mere days away from falling to ruin. The annual Weird Livestock Showcase always delivered on the promise of its name, with two-headed calves and goat-eyed pigs. And sure as sugar, local homemaker Nana Faye's mincemeat pie would win the coveted blue ribbon from the fair's amateur bake-off competition.

Nana Faye's pie was so renowned that the bake-off's judges volunteered years in advance. Being on the panel was the only guaranteed method for getting a slice of pie.

For as many years as Nana Faye won the blue ribbon, she worked to keep the recipe secret. She would sidestep questions from reporters, decline to contribute to the bake-off's charity recipe book, and refuse to entertain offers from regional bakeries willing to pay for her culinary secrets.

Upon Nana Faye's death, she bequeathed the recipe—along with forty-two blue ribbons—to her only child, Mortimer Wright. Mortimer had racked up significant gambling debts, so despite his pledge to keep the recipe in the family, he sold it to local entrepreneur Bettie Aster within days of his mother's funeral. Bettie launched a major regional ad campaign the day before she put the pies up for sale at her Five Points storefront, Bettie's Boulangerie.

But something was wrong with the pies. Customers complained about stomachaches and nausea. Bettie threw out the remainder of the first batch, fearing a bacterial problem, and made a new batch from scratch.

These pies were worse. Customers who ate them lost teeth and fingernails. Their hair came out in clumps.

Bettie suspected that Mortimer had conned her with a phony recipe. She attempted to file a lawsuit against him, but to no avail. Mortimer had been found dead that very morning. The cause of death was an obstruction of the large intestine.

Somehow, Mortimer's digestive tract was full of blue ribbons.

10

Hazel felt a rising tide of dread as they neared the hospital. The terror of her run-in with the monster the previous night hadn't left her; she could feel it buzzing under her skin, so that even when she turned her mind to other things, the fear was still with her.

Fine, she thought to herself. *If you can't shake it, then use it. Transmute it. Fear into resolve. Heartbreak into anger.*

It was worse, somehow, knowing that the hospital was connected to the killings. Despite the toll her mom's job had taken on her, Hazel had always considered the place a site of hope and possibility. People said miracles happened there. But if that were true, they were ordinary miracles. The stuff of hard-working people just trying to do good.

Leave it to the Yellow Court to tarnish that.

Whatever else Hazel and her friends might find, at least Hazel's mom wouldn't be caught up in it. She was finally off duty; Hazel had made sure she was sleeping soundly before she left. In the note she left behind, she made no mention of the hospital, only saying that she was spending the day with her friends.

Serena tensed up just outside of the main entrance. "Hold on," she hissed. "Do you guys *feel* that?"

"Spooky sense?" asked Emrys.

"Big-time," confirmed Serena.

Hazel's skin prickled, but there was nothing supernatural about it. "Not me," she said.

"Or me," said Emrys. "Are you sure—"

He dropped the question at a withering glance from Serena.

"There's definitely something here," Serena said, and despite herself, Hazel felt a little thrill of validation.

"I knew it," she said.

Serena massaged her temple. "You guys really don't feel this? What gives?"

"It is likely connected to your particular sensitivity," said Van Stavern.

"I'll never get used to being called *sensitive*," Serena muttered.

"There's precedent for it," said Van Stavern. "Some of the Order have always been especially sensitive to the presence of otherworldly powers. The clairvoyants among us."

"What, like fortune tellers?" said Serena.

"More like mediums," said Van Stavern. "Those to whom the boundary between worlds is less of a wall and more of a veil."

Hazel shrugged. "You do have a problem with boundaries," she said.

"Laugh it up," Serena groused. "I can't believe out of all of us, I'm the one who's most tuned in to the creepy radio waves. There really is no justice in this world, is there?"

"Yeah," said Hazel somberly. "Poor Clara learned that the hard way."

Serena sighed. "Touché. No more complaints from me." She leveled a gaze at Hazel. "But let's consider ourselves warned. There's something dangerous inside this building. You sure you want to go through with this?"

No. Not in a million years. Hazel was too young and too scared and way too exhausted to attempt to hunt a supernatural hunter. But want to or not, it was what they had to do. By now, Hazel was used to playing the adult because there wasn't anyone else around to do it. To quietly taking care of things in the background. This was no different.

She nodded, and they set off toward the hospital entrance together.

✕

At the elevator bank, Hazel was surprised to see a familiar face. Even more surprising was how the face lit up at the sight of her.

"Hazel!" said Nisha. "And . . . Serena? Are you friends?"

"Best friends," answered Serena. "Are you friends?" This was directed at Hazel, who blushed.

"Not really," she said.

"Not yet," said Nisha. "But it's inevitable, seeing as we can't get enough of this place."

She leaned in closer to Hazel and stage-whispered, "It's the vending machines, right? I love them, too."

Hazel giggled, and Serena gave her a weird look. She supposed she didn't giggle much.

"Emrys, Nisha," said Serena, by way of introductions. "We go to school together. She's a friend of my brother's. But don't hold it against her."

"Hey, what can I say? We kids of the rainbow need to stick together."

"The rainbow?" Emrys asked.

"My mom is trans," Nisha explained, and she pointed to two colorful iron-on patches on her tote bag. One had stripes of light pink and powder blue, with a white stripe down the middle; the other's stripes were deeper shades of pink, purple, and blue. Hazel recognized the first as the trans pride flag.

Nisha shrugged. "When you're the two Brown kids with queer parents at a very white, very traditional private school, you learn to have each other's backs."

"Except there's three of us," Serena pointed out.

"So hang out with us," Nisha said breezily. "Your brother's cooler than you know."

"What's this one?" Hazel asked, and she brushed her fingers against the unfamiliar patch.

"Bi pride," Nisha said, and she smiled. "That one's for me."

Hazel blushed again, although she wasn't sure why. Maybe she felt silly for not recognizing the flag, or for touching it without asking first.

Serena gave her another look, which only deepened her blushing.

"Maybe we *should* hang out, Nisha," Serena said, although her eyes lingered on Hazel as she said it. "Are you volunteering today?"

"Clocking out," Nisha said. "I've got my hours for the week. Fair warning: Dr. Strathmore is especially frazzled today." She stepped aside as the elevator behind her dinged. "Nice meeting you, Emrys. Hazel—I like your headband." With that, she was gone, and the three friends filed into the elevator.

"She seemed nice," said Emrys.

"But why did she mention my headband?" Hazel asked. "Do you think she could tell something's off about it? Maybe she saw through the disguise?"

"It was a compliment," Serena said with a smile, bumping Hazel with her shoulder. "Don't read too much into it."

Hazel couldn't promise that.

✕

Nisha had been right about the doctor's mood. Strathmore seemed nearly frantic. He'd probably been working many hours already, maybe even overnight. Hazel knew that the doctors' work schedules weren't any more forgiving than her mother's, and Strathmore had always seemed especially dedicated.

When he buzzed into the waiting room, three different nurses immediately beelined for him, peppering the doctor with questions. He answered quickly, then turned his eyes to the young volunteers.

"Are you all new? I don't have time to give you the tour, but . . . Hazel?"

Suddenly Dr. Strathmore seemed to come to, his autopilot disengaging.

"I didn't know you'd started volunteering," he said with a smile. "That's wonderful! How the heck are you?"

"I'm good!" Hazel said, as brightly as she could manage. Hopefully it did something to combat the dark circles under her eyes.

"You know your mom is off today, right?" Dr. Strathmore laughed. "What am I saying? Of course you do. We're happy to have you on board, though. And since you already know your way around, that'll be a huge help. I'm afraid we're a bit overwhelmed today."

"Put us wherever you need us," Hazel said.

The doctor nodded, glancing down at his clipboard. "No phones today, please," he said, getting right to business. "Not if you want me to sign off on your hours."

Hazel resented the suggestion that they were only there for the credit. But then she remembered that they weren't exactly being honest about their intentions.

On his application, Emrys had written that he "wanted to help people" by using his "unique skillset." *That* was true enough.

The doctor pointed at Serena. "Can you collect lunch trays in the cafeteria? It's a sticky job, so you'll want to wear gloves." He turned to Emrys. "And you look like a reader. You can be on mail sorting."

"Actually," said Serena, "we were hoping to stay together."

Dr. Strathmore shook his head. "Sorry, kids," he said. "No can do. As I mentioned, we're stretched pretty thin. Hazel here can round up wheelchairs." His gaze returned to his clipboard. "They end up all over the place, but that shouldn't be a problem for you. Don't forget to check the bathrooms."

A garbled message sounded from the ancient intercom. Hazel couldn't make out much, but she heard Dr. Strathmore's name clearly.

"Gotta run," he said. "Don't forget to check out when you're finished!" With that, he hurried past them and down a narrow hallway.

"I can't believe he's splitting us up," Emrys said.

"It's fine," said Hazel. "It doesn't change anything. We'll meet up when our shifts are over, and then the real plan can begin."

The plan, as it was, was for Hazel and her friends to sign out of their volunteer shifts, then slip into a quiet space and await nightfall. Hazel would then linger in one of the hospital's recovery wings alone, providing a tempting target for any heart-stealing monsters.

In truth, however, Emrys and Serena would be hidden nearby, watching Hazel through Serena's mirrored shield. If Van Stavern was to be believed, Serena's bond with the Aegis of Truth *should* allow her to see through any illusions, alerting them to the relic's true form. Then, if it came to blows, Emrys would use his weirdlight to destroy it, just as he'd done with the Wandering Hour.

Hazel's job wasn't glamorous, but it was vital. And until she grew into her own relic, then she'd just have to console herself with being the team strategist—as well as their bait.

Luckily, her volunteer duties provided her the most unrestricted access to the hospital. Collecting wheelchairs gave her a fine excuse to snoop around while she counted down the hours. Hazel roamed the hallways, not worrying too much about stray wheelchairs. The building buzzed with activity, as it always did. Visitors clutched flowers, stuffed animals, and mylar balloons; looking past the colorful gifts, Hazel could see that many people appeared tired and scared. Her mom always said that caring for patients was only half her job; the other half was about caring for the people who loved those patients. Doctors rarely had time to consider the complicated storm of emotions these people were navigating, so it fell to the nurses to guide them through the tempest.

Her mom also liked to add that the third half of her job was about managing the doctors themselves. When Hazel had been little, the joke had driven her to distraction. Three halves was impossible! Of course, that had been her mom's whole point. The job required more of her than she could possibly give.

Hazel found herself heading downstairs, back to the basement level where she'd encountered Worthmann. She still didn't *want* the man to be involved in all this mess, but if he was, then perhaps he'd left behind some sort of clue.

But all she found was the same supply closet she'd seen the day before.

There was, however, a door leading to another stairway. This stairway went down even farther than the main stairwell. Was there a *sub*-basement? Why wouldn't it be more accessible?

At the base of the staircase was a dimly lit landing and a heavy metal door. Hazel pushed it open, and she was greeted with a blast of cold air and fluorescent light. There was a vaguely familiar scent in the air. She'd smelled it at school the day they'd dissected frogs. Formaldehyde?

Hazel realized all at once where she was. The smell, and the cold, and the stainless-steel gurney in the center of the room; the walls lined with steel cabinets. She was in the hospital morgue!

She crossed to the center of the room, morbidly curious. There was a drain set in the concrete floor—for cleaning up messes?—and a freestanding scale beside the gurney. She knew from TV that organs were removed and weighed during an autopsy. It was just like the old Egyptian myth, where the gods of the afterlife judged a mortal by the heaviness of their heart.

Suddenly, her eye began to buzz.

Hazel realized she was exactly where she shouldn't be: alone in an off-limits area, where her friends would never know to look for her. Surrounded by *corpses* that were just out of view. She shuddered against the cold and hurried back the way she'd come—

But the door was closed.

Had *she* done that somehow? Had someone *else* sealed it from the outside? Hazel searched for a handle. With even that she could retreat to the Blue Reliquary using the Portam Charm. But there was nothing. Just a flat pane of steel.

Hazel pounded on the metal; it was cold to the touch, and too thick. Hitting it as hard as she could barely made any sound at all.

She pulled out her phone to text her friends. She had no service, not even the hospital's Wi-Fi. She was too far underground.

Buried alive, with only the dead to keep her company.

The Midtown Mummy 🔒

From the New Rotterdam Wiki Project

Anyone who grew up in New Rotterdam in the 1980s and 1990s can recall the horrifying, shriveled face of the Midtown Mummy, which was on display in the Founders' Museum of History and Technology during that era. A source of endless curiosity—and just as many ghost stories—the desiccated human corpse evoked images of ancient Egypt at its grandest. But this mummy was no pharaoh unearthed from a booby-trapped tomb by daring archaeologists. It was found by a group of teenagers playing hooky in an abandoned warehouse in downtown New Rotterdam.

While scientists puzzled over where the corpse had come from, popular rumor laid the blame on the horse-sized spiders long believed to inhabit the New Rotterdam Sewers. This rumor is largely believed to have started because the warehouse had been festooned with cobwebs. Scientists who examined the mummy found no evidence of puncture marks, however, and a hastily organized series of militia-led sewer safaris did not turn up any sign of spiders, although the excursions were not uneventful.

Despite its continued popularity among museum guests, a vocal segment of concerned citizens, led by a local PTA, insisted that the museum had acted inappropriately in displaying an unidentified corpse of indeterminate age. With their fundraising efforts threatened, the museum board voted in 1997 to inter the mummified corpse at Abaddon Hill Cemetery.

In 2005, advances in DNA technology and a popular online petition led the New Rotterdam Police Force to reopen the case. It was decided that the Midtown Mummy would be exhumed from its grave so that it could be subjected to DNA testing and, finally, identified.

To the shock of all assembled, including a visibly distraught reporter for WROT-13, the grave was found to be empty.

The whereabouts of the Midtown Mummy remain unknown.

11

Someone was bound to come and find Hazel, she was sure. She only had to wait patiently.

She continued banging on the door, hoping to catch the attention of some passerby, or maybe a nurse entering the basement for fresh supplies.

But as the hours ticked by and her hammering continued to go unanswered, Hazel's surety of a rescue grew softer. Her hopefulness moved through the various states of matter—solid to liquid; liquid to vapor.

Then six o'clock came and went without anyone finding her—the check-out time for her volunteer shift—and Hazel knew she was in trouble.

Serena and Emrys must be beside themselves, but without a way to contact them, Hazel wasn't convinced they'd find her on their own. They didn't know the hospital like she did, and even she'd been surprised by the well-hidden morgue.

Hazel looked around, studying the dreary room. The stones here were just as old as in the room where she and Worthmann had spoken. Part of the original building, then? She supposed it made sense that they'd keep the cadavers in a low, cool place, separate from the rest of the hospital. And if Worthmann had been exploring unnoticed by the staff, he'd no doubt have found the morgue eventually. What else might he have discovered down here?

Hazel moved away from the door, investigating the room. There wasn't much to it, truth be told. A bland, white-tiled floor offset the venerable stone bricks that enclosed the space. Hazel pried open one of the steel cabinets lining the walls and was greeted by rows of clinical jars filled with blue liquid. FORMALDEHYDE 37%, read the bottles in big bold letters, followed by the chemical formula: CH_2O.

Hazel inspected the gurney at the center of the room, but even that was fairly featureless. Just a steel frame made mobile by four black wheels, topped with clean white hospital bedding.

Closing her eyes, Hazel attempted to connect to her spooky sense. How had Serena described it? *Tuned in to the creepy radio waves.* Hazel may not be as sensitive to the otherworldly as her friends, but perhaps she could use that description to get a read of the place. Turn the metaphorical radio dial until she found a signal.

She moved slowly around the circumference of the morgue, her fingertips lightly touching the cabinets, the stone walls, and finally the mortuary coolers that stored the cadavers. She kept her eyes half-lidded, her thoughts quiet, listening for the telltale buzz.

Her fingers had just touched one of the coolers when she felt it.

The pressure was accompanied by a shock of cold and a throbbing pulse that Hazel felt in her chest. All of a sudden, her heart was racing.

Her heart . . .

Hazel opened her eyes. Something was in that cooler.

Grimacing, she took a step back. She knew cadavers were just that—the bodies of people who had expired at the hospital, awaiting burial or cremation. They were lifeless tissue, every bit as menacing as a hamburger. Right?

Hazel wasn't so sure anymore. Where the Doomsday Archives were concerned, even ordinary objects could hunt and kill. What might a corpse infused with the otherworldly do?

She pressed her ear to the steel pane and listened. At first there was nothing. Then, a quiet thump, followed by another and another. It sounded like a beating heart. Hazel leaned back, casting her eyes to the sealed doorway. Perhaps this was why the door had been closed behind her. Perhaps whatever had killed Clara was in here even now.

But Hazel didn't think so. The thing that had found her last night was a different sort of predator. It used *hope* to trap its prey, drawing its victims in with pretty lies.

Her fingers shaking, Hazel took hold of the cooler handle, then pulled it open with a grunt.

Inside, the cooler was empty.

Hazel breathed a sigh of relief. No dead body, then. But as she peered into the dark recess of the coffer, she saw *something* looming at the far end, obscured by darkness. Whatever it was, it had set off Hazel's sixth sense.

Taking a deep breath—and casting yet another nervous glance back at the sealed door—Hazel crawled inside.

The cramped space was even colder than the morgue. Hazel's whole body began to shake, whether with fear or chill or both, she couldn't tell. She inched forward on her stomach and elbows, fighting the tide of panic that was rising with every moment in this thing. This must be what it was like to be buried alive.

No. No, she couldn't think like that, or the fear would win.

Transmute fear into resolve, she told herself. *Heartbreak into anger.*

Hazel pulled her arm free, stretching it toward the dark shape at the end of the cooler. This deep, there was almost no light to see by. Her fingers grasped at air. Just another inch . . .

Finally, she brushed against something cold and solid. Hazel snatched at the object, finding purchase on a surface that felt like wood. She dragged it back toward her, then scrambled out of the cooler as quickly she could, her breath coming out in ragged gasps.

She glanced down to find the object in her hands was an ornate lacquered box. It looked old: nineteenth century, at a guess. And carved into the lid was a strange, smiling face. A mask, Hazel realized.

Her mind went to the story of the deadly mummers' play. It *had* to be connected.

She slowly opened the box to find a velvet interior, the cloth a rich yellow. There was an inset to the lining where an object might rest, and Hazel thought that it would be perfectly shaped for a mask. Tucked into the velvet was a paper card, its back decorated with a golden chess piece topped with a regal cross.

A yellow king.

Hazel turned the card around.

Resurrection is possible, the card read, *but only with sacrifice. Don the mask and it will guide you. Pay the mummers' price, and the doctor will perform his miracle.*

A gift from the Yellow Court.

A chill ran up Hazel's spine. So this *had* been the work of the Court. Just as Van Stavern warned, they'd dropped a relic right into Saint Azazel, knowing the havoc it would cause.

Serena was right. Worthmann must be the killer. Whatever he'd been before, the relic had turned the man into a monster. And now he was using the hospital morgue as his base of operations. Hazel had to warn Emrys and Serena.

But first she had to escape the morgue before he came back for *her*.

×

Hazel approached the thick steel barrier as she would any other problem—scientifically.

She knocked against the metal, listening to the way it muted the sound. The pane was thick. Very thick. And the fact that it was steel presented both a problem and an opportunity.

Steel itself wasn't a base element, not like iron or carbon. Rather, it was an alloy combining the two under high heat, along with a handful of other materials. This made it complicated to transmute using the Magnus Crown. Base elements, or even the chemical compounds made by them, she might be able to adjust by adding or subtracting electrons from the mix. But steel was way too complex to think of as a chemical formula. She'd need to find another way to get through it.

Hazel thought back to her research on the philosopher's stone and the secrets of alchemy. It was all such a muddle, science and mysticism blending into something every bit as opaque as a steel slab. What was real, and what was fantasy? What were the rules? Van Stavern had said that ancient alchemists hoped to elevate the soul by elevating matter. Right now, Hazel needed to do the opposite. Elevating *her* soul required tearing this door down.

The ancient alchemists had been preoccupied with creation, but equally potent was the philosopher stone's potential for destruction.

Aqua fortis.

All of a sudden, it came to her. Albert Magnus's formula that could dissolve any metal but gold. She thought back to the information she'd read while using her mom's laptop. In her research of alchemy, Hazel had turned both to conjury *and* chemistry, and the phrase *aqua fortis* had appeared in both. It was another name for nitric acid, an incredibly potent compound that could indeed eat through most metals—including steel. Nitric acid was composed of hydrogen, nitrogen, and oxygen, three elements readily available in the air. Normally, the creation of such a volatile compound would require intricate lab equipment. But if Hazel could use the Magnus Crown to bring those elements together into the structure she wanted, was it possible that she could create *aqua fortis* out of thin air?

It would be the most complex and dangerous working of alchemy she'd ever attempted. Certainly it would use a great deal of her stamina to make enough to melt through the door, and the fumes it gave off would be deadly toxic.

Hazel checked her phone. It was now 8 p.m. If Worthmann's pattern held, he was likely waiting until night to come and claim her. She didn't have much time.

Hazel thought of her mother, and how devastated she'd be if something happened to her. She couldn't end up like poor Clara. She had to survive, for her mom.

She pushed the gurney over on its side and threw the bedding into the far corner of the room, using the metallic stretcher as a shield. She peered over the top and focused her sight on the door's visible hinges. If she could just get through *those*, perhaps she could force it open.

Nitric acid. HNO_3. Hazel touched her fingers to her headband but found the Crown had already resumed its rightful shape, as if sensing it would be used. For the first time in their shaky partnership, Hazel swore it felt . . . eager.

Nitric acid, she commanded. *I need to burn through this door.*

But despite its sense of anticipation, the Crown didn't respond. The door remained inert.

What was she doing *wrong*? The more Hazel tried to control the thing, the more it seemed to resist her. It was like one of those joke finger traps that only drew tighter the more one struggled against them.

An urge for control and rationality can put one directly at odds with the unseen world.

Hazel recalled Van Stavern's warning from the previous day.

Remember: it is the hand that grips most tightly to the reins that suffers injury when those reins are yanked away.

Hazel sighed. She was used to solving her own problems, largely because she had to. Growing up poor, with a mother who worked endless hours just to keep them afloat, Hazel didn't have much of a choice.

It wasn't in her nature to lean on others. To ask for support. To let go.

But that was exactly what she needed, wasn't it? Especially where the Doomsday Archives were concerned. Hazel *couldn't* solve these problems on her own. She thought of the presence she sensed within the Crown, a presence she'd been attempting to wrestle for control. Perhaps it was time to take a different approach—one of mutual partnership.

Perhaps it was time to let go of the reins.

"Please," she said, closing her eyes. "I need help. I don't know what to do. Can you show me?"

Something changed. Hazel opened her eyes, and a red glow occluded her vision, shining from within the Crown's bloody stone.

It came to her instantly. Not just the chemical formula, or even a visualization of the compound's molecular bonds. It was *understanding*—as true and pure as anything Hazel had ever experienced. In that moment, she saw the world for what it really was, the glittering strings that held the very air together. And she knew how to weave those strings into what she needed.

Focusing on the door, Hazel pulled and plucked, watched as molecules danced impossibly from their skeins and reformed into a new tapestry. Emrys had described his first working of the weirdlight a bit like this. He said a dazzling light seemed to peer from beyond a glittering curtain. Hazel could just see the light he mentioned, but that wasn't what held her interest. She needed the curtain itself.

The Crown was a patient tutor. It guided her as she worked. She became absorbed by her task, by the beauty and intricacy of her weaving. And it seemed to marvel at her ingenuity, making only small adjustments the further she went.

And then, almost too soon for Hazel, the work was done. The Magnus Crown gave her what amounted to a satisfied nod. Whatever test it had just imparted, she'd apparently passed. The strings dimmed, the curtain fading away.

And looming before Hazel were the bubbling remains of a charred and melted door.

Creeping Ginny

From the New Rotterdam Wiki Project

No sleepover is complete without a dare, and few dares have stood the test of time like the Creeping Ginny challenge, which has been a source of dread and fascination for New Rotterdam's children for generations.

The dare is simple, which may account for its enduring popularity. To complete it, a child must stand alone before a window in a darkened room; while the window should remain closed, any curtains or blinds must be left open. The child lights a candle, then turns in a circle while reciting a short verse.

Some sources report additional details and direction, such as the number of rotations the child should make, whether their eyes should remain shut or focused on the flame, or even the placement of bread crumbs along the windowsill.[1] Despite such variations, the verse itself is always the same:

> *Creeping Ginny, are you lost*
> *Creeping Ginny, in the frost*
> *Let my candle be your guide*
> *Creeping Ginny, come inside*

After performing the ritual, the child is meant to remain in the dark, staring out the window and awaiting the arrival of "Creeping Ginny," most commonly described as a spectral child with blue lips, pallid cheeks, luminous eyes, and a nose blackened with frostbite.

Many children claim to have seen a glimpse of the specter before running from the room in fright. At least some of these sightings can be attributed to clever pranksters lurking outside a friend's window, waiting for the right moment to leap into view. While generally harmless, such pranks are not always free of consequence.[2] Still, most agree that "Creeping Ginny" is a perfectly safe children's game.

Others point to the mysterious death of Meredith Bartholomew as evidence that there may be more to the legend. Meredith, age 12, was found dead of hypothermia in her bed one balmy July morning in 2009. Her window had been left open, but as the nighttime temperature had not dropped below 75 degrees, the coroner was at a complete loss to explain the girl's apparent cause of death.

The case remains unsolved, but leaked crime scene photos reveal two intriguing details: Meredith had left a candle burning by her bedside and bread crumbs spread out along her windowsill. Had she invoked Creeping Ginny in the night? If so, it was the last thing she ever did.

References

1. Rodrigo, Amee (2003). *Folk Stories and Cautionary Tales of New England.* Acheron University Press.
2. Kerrigan, Joseph (13 November 1993). "Child's Prank, Dropped Candle to Blame for Suburban Inferno." *New Rotterdam Watcher.*

12

Hazel ran.

Well, perhaps *ran* was putting it generously. Whatever trance had befallen her in working such a devastating act of alchemy, it had also drained her of nearly all her strength. Hazel's stomach was a knot of hunger. Her limbs screamed with every step.

Rising from behind the gurney's protective barrier, she'd nearly collapsed from dizziness right there in the morgue. Only her fear now propelled her forward—and her elation, if she was being honest.

She still couldn't quite believe what she'd accomplished with the Magnus Crown's power. Sure, in the past she'd nudged some elements back and forth on the periodic table, but this was an entirely different game. Had she really just reduced a solid steel door into a hissing lump of metal from halfway across the room? It seemed impossible. It was impossible! But for once, the impossible was working for *her*. Hazel couldn't wait to tell Emrys and Serena.

The thought of her friends drew her back to the present, however. As Hazel hurried from the isolated basement and into the hospital's recovery wing, where she and the others were supposed to meet, she was struck by a sense of wrongness. For one, the lights were dimmed nearly to black. Hazel knew this wing of the hospital dimmed the hall lights after 9 p.m., but never this dark, and certainly not this early.

Second, the hallways were strangely empty. Even at night, there were always beeping monitors and harried nurses rushing about. A hospital like this never truly slept. Yet the farther Hazel moved, the more she got the sense that the busy wing had been abandoned. Saint Azazel was . . . quiet.

She paused to peer into a patient's room, squinting into the shadows. It was so dark, at first Hazel assumed that the room was unoccupied.

But then she saw the silhouette of a person peering back at her from the darkness.

Hazel scrambled back, pulling out her phone. She quickly turned on the flashlight and pointed it forward.

A nurse stood in the center of the room, grasping a patient's chart. But he wasn't looking at Hazel. His eyes were blissful and unfocused, staring into some distance Hazel couldn't see.

Frowning, Hazel crept into the room. She waved her hand in front of the nurse's face. He was in some kind of trance. Then she glanced toward the patient lying in the bed. It was an old man and he was . . .

Oh no. The man was dead!

Worthmann's here. Every hair on Hazel's neck stood suddenly on end.

The victim's eyes were wide open, a look of joy stretching across his lined face. If Hazel had to guess, the man's heart was likely missing.

Just as Worthmann had used the Yellow Court's relic to lure out Clara with euphoric illusions, he was now using the mask to subdue the staff and patients of the hospital. That meant no one was safe, least of all her.

She snuck into another recovery room and found another dead patient, her face bright with delight. It was so utterly cruel, using hope to kill.

But Hazel hadn't realized Worthmann's relic could affect this many people. Had the mask always been so powerful? She remembered the note from the Yellow Court. *Pay the mummers' price, and the doctor will perform his miracle.* Perhaps with sacrifices, the relic grew in potency. But to what end? The note had mentioned something about a resurrection. Was Worthmann attempting to bring someone back from the dead?

Glancing at her phone's screen, Hazel saw she had nearly three dozen missed notifications. Emrys and Serena had indeed been panicked by her disappearance, then.

Still at hospital, she typed in a flurry. *Worthmann trapped me in basement.*

HE'S HERE! she added.

Hazel hurried along, listening carefully for any sound that might indicate Worthmann was stalking the halls. But then she saw a door she recognized, and she paused.

It was the room where she'd met Nisha, when the girl was reading to that coma patient from yesterday. Hazel wasn't totally sure what made her stop. She didn't feel a buzz from her spooky sense, and she wasn't especially excited to see another poor victim of Worthmann's.

But then she heard a quiet beep from inside, and another. Hospital equipment, humming dutifully along. That meant the coma patient was still alive.

Hazel raised her flashlight to the doorway and saw the pale woman lying supine in her bed. She couldn't say what drew her in, but Hazel found herself approaching the gurney. At its foot was a medical chart, with notes printed in clear, crisp writing. Hazel lifted the clipboard and read the name at the top.

STRATHMORE, MARY

How's your sister? Her mom's voice came to her instantly.

No progress yet, Dr. Strathmore had replied. *But I'm still hopeful.*

If anyone can break through, it's you.

Hazel scanned down the chart.

SUDDEN CARDIAC ARREST . . . LIFE SUPPORT BEGUN PER NEXT OF KIN . . .

Then, under the most recent date: ORGANS NO LONGER FUNCTIONING INDEPENDENTLY.

Resurrection is possible, but only with sacrifice.

Hazel's blood ran cold. Worthmann wasn't the killer.

Dr. Strathmore was.

She needed to find the others and regroup. They'd had this all wrong. Was it possible they were waiting for her in the Blue Reliquary? If so, then they wouldn't receive her texts.

It was worth checking, if only for the momentary bit of sanctuary. Hazel hurried from the recovery room and scanned the hallway for any closed doorways to make use of the Portam Charm. She spotted one a few feet away and rushed toward it, when suddenly another door farther down the hall creaked open.

She nearly screamed—until she saw Emrys's worried eyes peering from around the doorframe.

"Hazel!" he hissed, in what was probably meant to be a whisper. "Where in the world have you *been*?"

He'd emerged from a broom closet, and was quickly joined by Serena, who stepped out from around him. The sight of her friends was like a sip of warm cocoa on a cold, blustery night. Hazel felt her exhaustion more keenly than ever. She could barely stand.

"We hid when we couldn't find you," Serena explained. "We knew you'd never leave without us."

Emrys peered around nervously. "We need to get out of here. Come on, we'll hide out in the Blue Reliquary until it's safe!"

Hazel nodded, limping forward. This was the right call. She was in no shape to face Strathmore head on, even with her newfound proficiency with the Crown. In the reliquary, they could rest and plan.

"We already grabbed your backpack!" Serena said.

Hazel faltered, her feet slowly grinding to a halt.

Backpack? No, something wasn't right. Hazel squinted at the shape clasped in Serena's hands, a sleek and stylish faux-leather bookbag. She felt an itch of discomfort. A familiar pressure fluttered beneath her skin.

That backpack was wrong.

All of this was wrong.

Then, finally, she sensed the buzz screaming behind her right eye. Her spooky sense, ringing every alarm bell it could. How had she missed it?

Emrys disappeared first. His big, worried gaze melted instantly into the shadows. Then Serena's body was gone, taking with it the traitorous backpack. Only her face remained, hanging in the air, her smile wide and wild.

Serena's skin slowly peeled away, revealing not flesh and bone, but a hard, chitinous material molded into an ovoid shape that was only vaguely reminiscent of a human face. An uncanny light glowed from beneath its folds, putting Hazel in mind of an anglerfish.

It was a mask, but the most horrific mask she'd ever seen. And it hung from a neck stretched far beyond the limits of human anatomy. The mask dangled in the air, radiating its awful, unnatural light—a light that pulled at Hazel's heart even now.

The body attached to that mask was no longer human, though it had been once. Its limbs were long and knobbed, its arms and legs pulled to horrific proportions. The figure wore a white lab coat, the fabric now shredded along its seams and splattered with rusty brown stains. A battered stethoscope still hung from the figure's neck, lightly obscuring the name tag pinned to its chest. Hazel didn't need to read it to know what it said.

Dr. Strathmore.

The doctor had been fused to the mask, his skin inflamed where it joined with the relic's hard edges. And where his face should be—*had been*—only that awful light glared through.

How long had he been like this? Hiding in plain sight, concealing his disturbing transformation behind the mask's illusions. Or had the change come over him only tonight, as he fed his relic victim after victim in an effort to save his sister?

Hazel took a step backward, and the mask suddenly twisted in the air. The doctor's malformed posture shifted, his body alert.

Oh no . . .

He figured out she'd broken free of his illusions.

And with that thought, Strathmore came crashing forward, his distended limbs skittering across the linoleum floor.

Talk: The Last Mummers' Play 🔒

From the New Rotterdam Wiki Project

> This is the talk page for discussing improvements to the The Last Mummers' Play article.

> This is not a forum for general discussion of the article's subject.

But where are the ghosts?

Pardon me for questioning the wisdom of the mods, but as far as I can tell this is actual history—not an urban legend, creepypasta, or even an uncanny sighting. Does it really belong on this wiki? BlackthorneBabe (user) 10:56, 5 October [reply]

It's a fair question, BlackthorneBabe. Considering the connection to the de Ruiters, however, and the family's many strange acts in the city's history, we felt it merited mentioning. Added a "Legacy" section to clarify. LongNeckedDoug (user) 11:32, 5 October [reply]

It's actually kind of odd that there aren't more urban legends connected to the event. It's such a ghoulish story. Why isn't the doctor's ghost wandering the hospital searching for his missing heart and all that? KazooCadet (user) 09:43, 7 October [reply]

Kazoo, are you a psychic? Some girl just had her heart removed!! BlackthorneBabe (user) 18:34, 13 November [reply]

:)

Be careful what you wish for. It might just come knocking on your door. [user deleted] (user) 14:22, 10 October [reply]

And be careful what you post, creep. You are now on the banned list. LongNeckedDoug (user) 15:03, 10 October [reply]

13

Hazel raced down the corridor, and the creature followed.

It made no utterance as it gave chase—no primal scream or taunting laughter. Hazel didn't think it was even *breathing*. Its silence was an unnerving reminder that it was neither beast nor man.

The creature that had been Dr. Strathmore—the *Mummer*—defied categorization. It didn't belong, didn't *fit* in the world any better than it fit in Strathmore's skin, which it had pulled taut to the point of tearing.

Hazel choked back a sob. She couldn't waste the breath on crying. The Mummer was right behind her and closing fast. Mute as it was, its elongated, misshapen limbs beat out an irregular gait on the linoleum, like a diseased, arrhythmic heart.

And then there was the light. The eerie yellow-orange glow of the Mummer's lure shone at her back, casting her shadow ahead of her and cleaving it into a dark spectrum of silhouettes that seemed to writhe before her on the walls, the ceiling, and the floor. The darkness had been frightening but the light was far worse.

Hazel turned a corner, and the scrabbling behind her grew momentarily frantic as the Mummer's momentum sent it careening into the wall. It was faster than her, had been gaining on her steadily—but it was too big and too awkward to take turns gracefully. Every corner would buy her precious seconds. But would it be enough? Adrenaline was flooding through her, but it could only do so much to offset the toll the Crown had taken on her body. Her limbs shook with exertion; her stomach was a tight knot.

Hazel ignored the discomfort and the eerie dancing shadows and cast her gaze about for anything she could use. The corridor was lined with open doors, but each one was a dead end. Hiding wasn't an option, the Portam charm would take too long to cast, and she didn't have the first idea about what she could transmute that would stop the Mummer. The air? But the Mummer didn't appear to breathe, while Hazel herself was gasping for breath. The floor? But what even *was* linoleum?

The time she'd wasted making *gold*. Valuable and pretty and totally useless to her now. She cursed herself silently.

And then her whole body pitched forward, and she slammed against the ground.

The Mummer had her by the ankle. It scrabbled forward, pinning her to the floor and looming above her. Its eyes were still human, and they flashed with triumph from behind the chitinous mask. With its free hand, it held a scalpel—lightly, with the practiced skill of a surgeon—and it aimed the instrument at Hazel's heart.

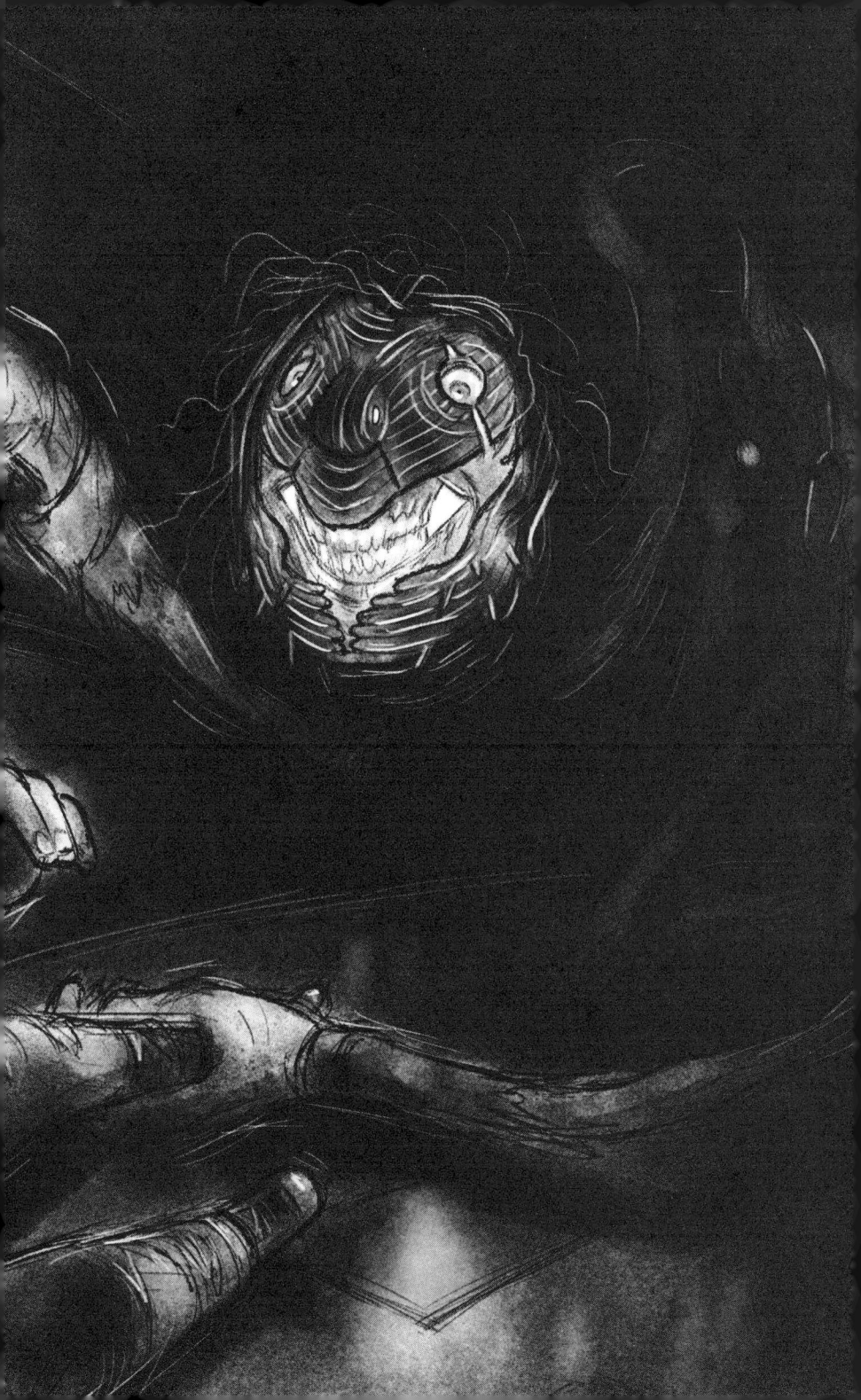

The philosopher's stone at her forehead answered the Mummer's luminous lure with a pulsing, ruddy glare of its own, and Hazel's vision shifted. She could once again see the binding threads of creation, ready to be rewoven. The scalpel was steel, as the morgue's door had been; she stuck with what she knew, pulling nitric acid out of the very air and reducing the weapon to a melted ruin.

But she didn't stop with the scalpel. The stethoscope around the Mummer's neck was made of steel, too.

The Mummer reeled back in shock and pain. The stethoscope bubbled and warped, gouging a line of molten trauma along the creature's clavicle. Still, it was silent; Hazel wasn't. Blades of pain pierced her gut, as the Crown demanded the blood price of its power.

She had to ignore it. The Mummer had let her slip from its grip. It writhed beside her on the floor, mad with pain, distended limbs thrashing. She wouldn't get a better chance to flee.

Hazel pulled herself shakily to her feet. She limped down the corridor. The stairwell was in view; she could take it down to the street or, even better, head directly to the reliquary. She was almost safe.

She passed a man who stood in an open doorway, swaying gently on his feet and staring off into space. Another fly caught in the Mummer's web, held hostage by his own desires. His face was wet with tears and lit with a beatific smile. Hazel spared a moment's thought for what the man was experiencing. Good news from a doctor? A loved one's miraculous recovery? Her heart heaved in sympathy.

In a world that seemed darker by the hour, hope was the one thing people couldn't do without. The Yellow Court had even turned Dr. Strathmore's hope against him, luring him in with the cruel promise of saving his sister. If they could poison hope itself, use it *against* people, then the world truly would be lost.

It wasn't enough to escape the Mummer. Hazel had to stop it.

She grabbed an IV stand, knocking the sac of fluid off the top and wielding it like a spear. She would pry the mask loose even if it meant taking off half the thing's head in the process.

The Mummer had fallen still. The melted steel had cooled, solidifying into an argent gash that leaked blood and pus onto the once-white lab coat. Hazel took a tentative step forward, then another. She extended the pole, looking for an exposed edge to the mask. She didn't dare make a sound. She wasn't sure how long the Mummer would remain unconscious, but she could hope—

Hope.

It had tricked her again.

The Mummer lunged forward with terrifying swiftness, effortlessly knocking the pole from Hazel's hands and gripping her by the throat. It hadn't even needed an illusion this time; playing possum had been enough to lure Hazel into its clutches.

Hazel gasped, gulping down a final breath before the monster's grip closed off her throat. She dug her nails into its clammy forearm, and its flesh came away in ribbons, but its grip only tightened. It flexed its free hand into a claw, rearing back to strike.

She had taken its scalpel. Now it seemed determined to end her with its bare hands.

"Hey, beautiful!" cried a voice. "Looked in the mirror lately?"

The creature snapped its head around, turning its ravenous eyes on Serena—and her mirrored shield. It reeled at the sight of its own reflection, dropping Hazel to block its eyes with its gnarled and bloody forearms.

"Hazel, come on!" cried Emrys from nearby. He extended a hand, but Hazel shrank from it.

"A-are you real?" she choked out.

Emrys appeared momentarily confused. "We heard you scream. We've been looking everywhere!"

Hazel didn't know if she could trust her eyes.

But she trusted her relic.

She looked again for the ethereal tapestry and the truth it showed. She saw the countless glittering threads that were Emrys, the ones that laced together into a pattern that was unique in all the universe. And she saw the threads that reached out from beyond his physical bounds to interweave with her own. This was Emrys, the real Emrys, *her* Emrys.

But as she watched, the pattern shifted. The skein came loose. Emrys himself went slack, and Hazel knew he'd fallen prey to the Mummer's vicious manipulations. The creature had recovered and turned its attention on Emrys; it was a spider and Emrys was both fly and web, unknowingly spinning his own inescapable trap from the threads of his most sacred and secret self.

Hazel couldn't abide that. Dr. Strathmore had been led to this place by desperation and hope. Like Hazel, he'd just wanted to protect his family. And like Hazel, he'd taken matters into his own hands in secret.

Unlike Strathmore, however, Hazel wasn't alone. She had friends she could rely on. Friends she wasn't about to let down.

The tapestry was fragile. Altering it took a deft and cautious hand—the careful skill of a weaver, or a surgeon.

This time, Hazel didn't bother being delicate. She turned her red gaze onto the tangled mess of organic molecules and fundamental forces and otherworldly *wrongness* at the heart of the Mummer. She sent a silent plea to the Magnus Crown, for one last bit of help. She felt the Crown give its approval—and she pulled.

Now, at last, the Mummer made a sound, shrieking at an inhuman register—but only for a second. And then its body was ripped apart before their very eyes, obliterated, its molecules scattering across the corridor like pearls flying loose from a broken necklace.

All that was left of the Yellow Court's abomination was an eerie, smoking mask. It clattered to the floor, and Hazel followed immediately after.

14

The next couple of hours were a flurry of activity. Apparently.

Hazel was unconscious for most of it.

Emrys and Serena had to recount their escape to her later, when they debriefed together in the reliquary. Following the destruction of the Mummer, Emrys quickly opened a door with the Portam Charm, while Serena dragged a senseless Hazel inside, closing the way behind them. Emrys then fled the hospital on foot, just as the staff and patients were coming to, and made it the rest of the way to 49 Eldridge Heights on his own.

Serena tended to Hazel while he traveled. Once Emrys arrived home, he opened another doorway into the apartment building, using the method Hazel had shown them in their experiments with the charm. Then he and Serena were able to rouse Hazel long enough to get her to her bedroom using her apartment key. Thankfully, Hazel's mom had stepped out to run some errands.

Though they were nervous leaving Hazel alone in her near-catatonic state, they fled the apartment before her mom returned. When she did, she found Hazel asleep in her bed.

"Snoring like a freight train," she told Hazel the next morning. "Honestly, I was impressed. Didn't know you had it in you."

But a worried look had crinkled her brow as she put a hand to Hazel's forehead. "You're warm. Are you feeling okay, honey? You don't look well."

Hazel had nodded and smiled at her mom. "Just a little tired," she said. "The sleepwalking took a lot out of me, I guess."

"Why don't you stay home from school today?" her mom suggested. "Recover a bit. I know it sounds corny, but self-care *is* important."

Hazel had to force herself not to laugh.

She pulled her comforter up, tucking it under her chin. "Thanks, Mom," she said. "I do think I need some rest."

Then, after a moment's hesitation, she continued. "Hey, Mom?"

"Yeah, baby?"

"I . . . there's this convention. RotterCon. Emrys and Serena really want to go. And I do, too. But the ticket is forty dollars. I've been trying so hard to come up with the money myself. I really have. I know things are tight right now. But no matter what I tried, I couldn't scrounge up the money. Do you think . . . maybe I could borrow some for a ticket? I'd pay you back, I promise."

"Pay me back?" A strange expression touched her mother's face, one that Hazel couldn't quite interpret. She wished she had a bit of Serena's clairvoyance right then.

"Oh, honey, I'm so sorry . . ." her mom said.

Hazel's heart sank. It had been too much. She should have known. She had known. She felt a wave of shame for even asking.

"*Of course* we can find the money for a ticket."

Hazel's eyes widened. Her mom brushed a lock of hair from her face.

"You're such a mature and resourceful kid," her mom continued. "It's easy to forget how much you take on. But you *are* still a kid, Hazel. I appreciate all you do, and I'm sorry I have to leave you alone so often. But let me be the parent occasionally, okay?" She winked. "It's actually kind of fun."

Hazel's eyes welled with tears. She couldn't help it.

"Baby!" her mom said, pulling her into a tight hug. "I'm so sorry if I made you think you have to carry this family all on your own. I'm here if you need anything, all right? Day or night. Even when I'm at work. You are my top priority."

Hazel pulled back, wiping the dampness from her eyes. "Thanks, Mom," she rasped.

Her mom's cell phone rang. She glanced toward it and frowned.

"My shift supervisor," she said. "But I'm already scheduled to work today." She grimaced worriedly toward Hazel.

"Answer it," Hazel said. "I'm all right."

Her mom nodded and rose from the bed, stepping out into the living room.

"What's up?"

Quite a bit, it turned out.

Though Hazel's mom had been scheduled to work that day, her supervisor told her not to come in. There had been an accident. The details were fuzzy, but several patients in the recovery wing had died overnight, likely due to a mysterious power outage. The hospital was conducting an internal investigation, but for now, Nurse Sheridan should hold tight.

Equally mysterious was the disappearance of Dr. Strathmore, who never returned to work following his shift the previous day. A staff member sent to check on the doctor found his apartment abandoned, the space cleaned of furniture and personal items. It looked like it hadn't been lived in for months.

Hazel's mom had grimaced when she heard the news. She put a hand over her mouth.

"Poor Strathmore," she said in a low voice. "It's always so sad when someone ghosts. This job is impossible. Sometimes people just . . . break."

So Hazel and her mom finally got their movie marathon. They spent the day in their pajamas, watching ancient romantic comedies set during the early days of email. It was evening before Hazel felt strong enough to venture back to the Blue Reliquary to join her friends.

She'd eaten nearly every edible morsel in her apartment. Using the Crown to destroy monstrous killers apparently required a lot of energy. Hazel asked Emrys and Serena if they had any snacks they could spare. Emrys brought two bags of chips, while Serena smuggled a pile of homemade cookies her dad had baked. Hazel devoured it all in moments.

She'd need to figure out a source of calorie-dense foods for the future, in order to safely use the Crown's powers. Thankfully, Serena had an answer at the ready.

"Dom's whole lacrosse team drinks these heinous protein shakes called Ultra Mass Gainz," she said. "They buy the powder in bulk, because it's cheaper that way. I could easily sneak you a tub now and then."

Hazel nodded. "Thanks," she said. "That should be perfect."

Emrys and Serena recounted how they'd hidden in the hospital as they searched for her, Serena's relic protecting them from the worst of the Mummer's powers while the rest of the staff and patients fell under its spell.

"Turns out this thing is pretty useful, after all," Serena said, tapping her nails against the mirrored shield.

"So what happened?" Emrys asked, looking at Hazel. The boy was practically vibrating in his seat. "With the Crown, I mean. Hazel, that was—you were amazing!"

Hazel described getting trapped in the morgue and her literal breakthrough in accessing the Magnus Crown's potential to demolish the steel door. She noted how that bit of news hadn't made it to her mom.

"Either they haven't found the mess yet," she guessed, "or someone is covering it up."

"You've already seen firsthand how these issues tend to resolve themselves as quietly as possible," said Van Stavern. "The Yellow Court is certainly involved, but the unseen world has its own ways of masking itself."

The tome let out an awkward cough. "Poor choice of words."

"Speaking of, at least we got the relic this time," Emrys said brightly. He indicated toward a plinth where a glass case had been erected around the Heart-Stealer Mask, as they'd come to call it.

Van Stavern had instructed Emrys and Serena in how to safely store the object, dulling its baleful power. Thankfully, the Order of the Azure Eye had left a number of such containers tucked away in the reliquary, the glass lined with silver and the plinths encircled with strange, apparently protective sigils.

Hazel glanced toward the thing, but then quickly averted her eyes. She still didn't like looking at the mask, warded or not.

"Indeed," intoned the Atlas, its blue orb swiveling across the table. It was hard to read Van Stavern's expressions with only a single eye to go by, but she thought she sensed pride in the sorcerer's gaze. "You've avenged a young woman, contained the relic, and unlocked the potential of a powerful tool for good. Well done, all. I daresay the old Order would be very pleased with what your Doomsday Archives has accomplished this day."

Emrys leaned back in his antique chair, staring up at the reliquary's cavernous ceiling. "Still," he said. "People died. And it was really scary. When the Mummer had me . . . The things it showed me felt so *real*."

"What did you see?" Hazel asked.

Emrys smiled bashfully, glancing back down at her. "If it's okay, I might keep that private."

Hazel nodded, though she couldn't help but notice that his eyes flicked toward Serena.

"One last thing before we finish," she said. "About RotterCon . . . I *do* want to go. And mom has agreed to get me a ticket. I hope you both still want to go *with* me?"

"Of course!" Emrys answered immediately.

Serena grinned at her. "A room full of sweaty horror nerds and deranged conspiracy theorists?" she said. "I wouldn't miss it."

Hazel smiled. "Thanks," she said. "I love you guys."

As the friends concluded their discussion, they gathered their things to return to their respective apartments. Hazel had brought her stack of chemistry books as usual, and she piled them into her backpack, along with the garbage from her snacking.

"Is that new?" Serena asked, taking in the chic, faux-leather bookbag. "It's *super* cute. Great taste."

Hazel brightened. "Thanks!" she said. Then she did a little twirl, and she and Serena laughed together.

It wasn't clear if Serena even recognized the gift that she herself had purchased, but Hazel found it didn't matter.

Though her family's financial situation hadn't changed, she vowed to accept help whenever it was given, banishing the specter of shame.

Transmute fear into resolve, Hazel told herself, *heartbreak into anger . . . and sorrow into hope.*

After all, in a world that seemed darker by the hour, hope was the one thing people couldn't do without.

New Article: The Heart-Stealer Mask 🔒

The page you searched for does not exist. To create the page, start typing in the box below (see the help page for more info). If you are here by mistake, click your browser's back button.

ⓘ *Content that __violates any copyrights__ will be deleted.*

B *I* ⚭ ▲ | > Advanced > Special characters > Help > Cite   ✎ ⌄

EPILOGUE

Hazel clicked through page after page of search results.

Just as he'd claimed, Julius Worthmann was not a celebrity. In fact, despite his billions, there was very little account of him at all in the local news. An article here about Saint Azazel's new pediatric wing. Another there about his more recent decision not to fund the ER, following the disappearance of its most respected surgeon.

Still, Hazel couldn't shake the feeling that Worthmann was connected to Dr. Strathmore's horrific transformation somehow. Perhaps, like Enoch Pierce, he'd been a clandestine agent of the Yellow Court all along, the very person responsible for putting the Heart-Stealer Mask into the doctor's hands.

If that was the case, he'd done an expert job covering his tracks. Hazel couldn't find any evidence to support the theory. It would remain a particularly nettlesome loose end.

But just before she gave up her inquiry, while scanning the seventh page of search results, Hazel did see something that caused her to pause. Her cursor hovered over a link to a local genealogy website.

Most of the page was partitioned behind a paywall. It was the kind of fancy academic site that charged big bucks for access to knowledge. But one short blurb had been made visible by Hazel's search parameters.

. . . led by interest from the Worthmann estate. Julius Worthmann, a local philanthropist and savvy businessman, is himself a descendent of the de Ruiters, the "founding family" of New Rotterdam. Worthmann funded several historical . . .

Hazel frowned. De Ruiter? Like Gideon de Ruiter, who her school was named after? And hadn't she seen that name somewhere else, too?

She opened the wiki page for the Last Mummers' Play. There! She was right. Lizbeth de Ruiter was the woman who'd died at Saint Azazel, setting off the tragic chain of events that led to the murder of an innocent man.

Interesting that Worthmann hadn't mentioned he was related to the very family who'd likely killed the doctor in his morbid tale.

Still, Hazel wasn't completely sure what to do with this information, beyond sharing it with Emrys and Serena. Something to keep in mind . . .

She closed the tab, taking a sip from the hot teacup resting beside her. Hazel yawned and stretched. It was getting late, but she had one other project she wanted to tackle tonight.

She brought her hand up to her hair, her fingers brushing over the filigreed lines of the Magnus Crown.

"You ready to get to work?" she whispered aloud.

The Crown didn't respond, of course. It couldn't talk—not like Van Stavern could, trapped as the sorcerer was in the *Atlas of the End*. But Hazel still felt a curious presence rouse from inside the relic. The invisible tutor was as eager to teach as Hazel was to learn.

Hazel opened a separate window, where several tabs were open, full of dubious information on ancient, mysterious arts.

"Okay," she said. "I am, too. So . . . how do we make a homunculus?"

ABOUT THE AUTHORS

Zack Loran Clark and Nick Eliopulos are best friends with a shared love of roleplaying games, epic fantasy, and spooky stories. Together, they are the authors of The Adventurers Guild trilogy. Separately, Zack is the author of *The Lock-Eater* and the Bleakwatch Chronicles series, and Nick has written nineteen officially licensed Minecraft books. Zack lives in Brooklyn, where he keeps a collection of potentially mystical artifacts. Nick lives in Upstate New York, just down the street from an allegedly haunted tavern. Thanks to the wonders of the internet, they still game together regularly.

The thrills continue . . .

Keep your eye out for
more adventures in

THE DOOMSDAY
ARCHIVES